PRAISE FOR REBEKAH'S WORK

HAVEN

"…the perfect balance of sexiness, action and angst." - Alexa Martin, author of INTERCEPTED

SATED

"…I LOVED IT. The book was respectful of geeks, people with disabilities, people of color, and the BDSM community, and it was informative and entertaining, and it was funny." - Carrie S, *Smart Bitches Trashy Books*

TREASURE

"This story is rich yet beguiling, magnificent yet down to earth, and intriguing yet heartwarmingly human." – J.J., *Rainbow Book Reviews*

SO SWEET

"Reading this novella made me happy. I'm definitely looking forward to more." - Lime Cello, *Heroes & Heartbreakers*

BOOKS BY REBEKAH

LOOSE ENDS
Rafe: A Buff Male Nanny

BEARDS & BONDAGE
Haven
Sanctuary

THE FIT TRILOGY (And Friends)
Fit
Tamed
Sated
Wrapped

SUGAR BABY NOVELLAS
So Sweet
So Right
So For Real

VAMPIRE SORORITY SISTERS
Better Off Red
Blacker Than Blue
Soul To Keep

STAND ALONE TITLES
The Fling
At Her Feet
Treasure

Rafe

• A BUFF MALE NANNY •

REBEKAH
WEATHERSPOON

For Doug

Chapter One

If she'd been paying closer attention, Dr. Sloan Copeland, M.D. would have noticed something was off the moment she pulled into the driveway. She never left the garage door open and neither did her live-in nanny, Tess, but that day, it was wide open and the contents of Sloan's complex storage system were on display for the whole neighborhood to see. The Chevy Tahoe Tess used to cart the girls around was there and nothing seemed to be missing when she stopped in front of the neatly arranged rack of garden tools. Still, she should have known.

It was only Wednesday, but the week already felt so long. Her six-year-old twins, Avery and Addison, were acting as if they could smell the end of summer and had started a comprehensive and coordinated boycott against bedtime. They'd even worked in musical numbers with some adorably ridiculous dance moves, but Sloan really would have appreciated that hour of sleep they'd managed to snatch from her with their scheming.

She'd loaded up on coffee and the tiny burst of adrenaline that always hit her system the moment she set foot in the ULA Medical Center, but after hours on her feet operating, she was desperate to get home and reset her system. She was grateful for the fact that Tess would keep the girls distracted long enough for Sloan to squeeze in a quick, hot shower.

Sloan cut the engine to her Mercedes, then hit the button on her garage door opener. Before she could grab her purse out of the passenger seat, the door at the top of the garage stairs opened just enough for Avery's small face to poke through. Sloan climbed out of the car and smiled at her daughter. "Hey, baby."

But instead of launching into a detailed description of everything that had happened since the moment she woke up, Avery tucked her lips between her teeth before ducking back into the house.

"Crap," Sloan said under her breath. She knew that look on Avery's face. She'd done something bad. It was a toss up between nearly maiming Addison and attempting to set something on fire, if Sloan had to take a guess.

"Hey, love bugs! Hey Tess!" she called out as she walked into the mudroom. No response as she stepped out of her shoes and pushed them under the bench. She could hear an episode of *My Little Pony: Friendship is Magic* coming from the TV room. Something was off, but Sloan still didn't catch it. The scene she was met with wasn't too unusual. Addison sat in the middle of the floor, a small bowl of green grapes in her lap. Avery was standing behind the far end of the couch bouncing on her heels.

"Hi, babies."

"Hi, Mommy! Hi," Avery blurted out before biting her lip again.

"Tess said I have to give you this as soon as you get home." Addison held up a piece of paper. Sloan set down her purse and took the folded COPELAND stationery out of Addison's hand.

"Where is Tess?" she asked as she opened the cream cardstock.

I'm sorry, but I quit.

"She left," Addison said.

Sloan blinked and read the note again. "Uh," was all that came out of her mouth. She swallowed and gave it another try as she looked between the girls. "Where's Tess?"

"Gone," Addison said.

"She's gone, Mommy. Gone!" Avery added.

A sudden, strange pressure gripped the temporal vein on the side of Sloan's face. "She what?" She kept her voice calm, but the pressure was quickly spreading lower, to her chest. Sloan got it then. Avery wasn't worried about her own screw up, she was hyped up over Tess flying the coop. Sloan flopped down on the couch and reached for Avery, who climbed over the arm instead of walking around.

"Baby, what time did Tess leave?" Avery was big on telling time these days.

"Three one eight." Sloan glanced at her smart watch. It was nearly seven.

"She's been gone for almost four hours?"

"Mhmm," Avery said with a deep nod.

"Why didn't you call me?" Sloan asked. She had the number to her office at the medical center programmed into the speed dial on the landline in the kitchen. Once the girls exhibited a reasonable understanding of how that phone worked and that it wasn't a toy, she told them which number to dial in the case of an emergency—if Tess couldn't help them.

Addison tilted her head back. "You said emergencies only and Tess said this wasn't an emergency. She said we could watch TV 'til you got home."

"She put all of her stuff in a pick-up truck," Avery said.

"What the—" Sloan hopped up and practically ran down the hall to Tess's wing of the house. Sure enough, all of her things had been cleaned out of the in-law suite. Drawers and closet completely empty. Toothbrush and toiletries gone from the ensuite bathroom.

"What in the fresh hell?" Sloan breathed.

"You said we couldn't say hell." Of course Avery followed her. Sloan turned around and scooped up her little girl.

"You're right. I'm sorry."

"This means we're going to get a new nanny, right?" Avery asked. "Kaydem has a new nanny."

"Yeah, I think that's what this means." Fuck. She just needed a few minutes. Just a few to scream into a couple of pillows. Maybe trash the place. Finding the girls a new nanny would be the first thing on her list. After she called the feds on Tess. "Are you hungry?"

Avery tipped her chin in a firm nod. "So hungry."

"Can you do something for me? Go ask Addison what she wants on her pizza. I'll be right there."

"Okay."

"Thank you." She pressed a hefty kiss to Avery's temple, then set her back down on the floor. "I will be there in just a few minutes."

Avery nodded, then turned and bolted down the hall. Once she was alone, Sloan realized she wasn't breathing right. Her full-time, live-in nanny had really just up and quit, and abandoned her freaking children in the middle of the day. No phone call. No text. Nothing. When her heart stopped racing, Sloan would grasp onto the silver linings, like how both Avery and Addison were perfectly fine even though they'd been left unsupervised for hours. That was the most important thing. They were okay. Sloan would focus on that, she really would, just as soon as she figured out just what the hell had happened to Tess.

•

"It's okay to cry. What she did was pretty fucked up."

"I'm not crying," Sloan huffed as she shoved the sheets she'd just torn off Tess's bed into the washing machine. She stood up and wiped the tears off her cheeks, then slammed the washer door shut. It was barely ten p.m., but she'd cycled through a whole bunch of emotions surrounding Tess and her unnecessarily over-the-top resignation. Sloan had ordered dinner and got the girls through their evening routine with relative ease, considering the day they'd had.

They were handfuls and a half, but they knew when Sloan had hit her emotional limit. She was tempted to press them for more information about Tess's departure, but decided against it, especially when they asked if Tess really wasn't coming back and if she didn't like them anymore.

Sloan wanted to box Tess in the street for leaving the way she did, but she really wanted to mess her up for making her children feel like they had done something wrong. Even if Tess hated Avery and Addison, Tess didn't have to pull this crap. Talk about unprofessional.

After the girls drifted off to sleep, Sloan tried calling Tess for a third time. Her first two attempts had been sent right to voicemail. She left messages and sent a few texts, and just as Sloan debated calling the police—Tess did have a boyfriend, and maybe he forced her to quit—a reply text popped up on her phone.

Child care just isn't for me. I'm sorry.
The keys to the house and the Tahoe
are in the basket.

Relief flooded Sloan for a few seconds until the truth settled in. Tess really had just up and quit with no warning and left Addison and Avery to deliver the news. Sloan knew there was nothing she could do. Even if begging were an option, she didn't want Tess's irresponsible ass back. Finding a new nanny for the girls as soon as possible was the priority now. She also knew she had to fill the twins' father in on what happened.

She did not want to speak to Drew about this. She knew exactly what he would say. That she and the girls should move back to Seattle. She could come work for him at his practice. His mom would watch the girls. They'd never be together again, so Drew would at least try to have his way and, at every turn, take his chance to remind Sloan she couldn't have it all.

The thought of even having to have a conversation with Drew? About the girls? That pushed her anger and frustration to a boiling point and, unfortunately for Sloan, her extreme emotions usually came with tears. She raged cleaned as much as she could and then, instead of calling Drew, she called her friend Xeni.

"Girl, cry it out," Xeni said. "Someone you trusted with your children and your home just up and ditched you. It's completely reasonable to be upset. Express that emotion. It's healthy. And when you're done and you feel like you can think more clearly, I just need to know what kind of hex you want me to put on this bitch when we find her."

Sloan laughed, but the tears still leaked down her face as she leaned back against the dryer. "Don't waste your magic on her. She isn't worth it."

"I know, but she has it coming. Or, I mean, you could leak me her address and then I'll just go have a chat with her."

"Yeah, that'll be great for your career. 'Local kindergarten teacher arrested after assault on former nanny'."

"I would just do the talking. You know I'd make a call for the heavy lifting."

Sloan chuckled some more. Xeni had six elderly aunts in South Pasadena just looking for a reason to get in a knife fight. "I appreciate the gesture, but no. Tell the Everly sisters I won't be needing their services."

"They can make it look like an accident, but fine. Whatever. You got the girls covered for tomorrow? I have meetings at school until one, but I can sit with them for a bit until you get home."

"No, it's okay. My neighbor's daughter is going to watch them 'til the end of the week. The girls love her, so at least I won't get too many complaints about this transition of power."

"Can you hire her full time?"

"No," Sloan sighed. "She goes back to college next week."

"Ahh man. Well, I'll help you tag team this. You ask around the hospital tomorrow and I'll ask up at school. I think between us we can find someone or at least link you up with a reliable agency."

"Yeah. Okay. Thank you."

"You know I got you, babe. You get some sleep. I'm gonna look up the street view of Tess's man's house and find the best entry points."

Sloan burst out laughing. "Will you stop?!"

"Never."

They finally said their goodnights and Sloan set about shutting down the house. She'd call her mother in the morning. Thanks to the time difference, her parents were already asleep back in Rhode Island. She should be too if she wanted to make it through the next day with a clear head. She headed upstairs, peeked in on the girls one more time and then made her way to her bedroom, where she called her ex-husband, Drew Ballos, the biggest asshole she'd ever met, M.D..

•

Rafe Whitcomb's day had just taken a turn. It had been three weeks since the Bakers had relocated to Sydney, Australia. He'd been taking care of their four kids for over six years. When Jill Baker was offered a job overseas, they jumped at the chance to provide their children with an international experience—her words, not Rafe's. They asked him if he wanted to come along; same pay, same perks, same schedule, just a different hemisphere.

Rafe was tempted. He'd been overseas with families he'd worked for before. Living abroad, even if he had to keep up with the Bakers' kids, would be a pretty cool experience. But when Chris Baker joked that the woman of Rafe's dreams could be waiting for him down under, a whole potential life flashed before his eyes and he wasn't sure he loved what he saw.

He'd been taking care of other people's children since he was seventeen. Being a full-time, live-in nanny didn't leave a whole lot of time for a social life, or a life of any kind. Most women he dated were fine with the fact that he was only free two nights a week and that those two nights were set in stone. 'Cause it was all so fucking cute, how good he was with kids. But when they realized that the kids really did come first, that being with Rafe meant their relationships would come with a lot of rain checks, they were out the door. And that was only if they didn't try to convince him to quit first.

Rafe didn't want to picture that shit happening halfway across the world. At some point he knew he was going to have to step away from this kind of intensive childcare. He still wanted to work with children, but he wanted more time for himself, so when the Bakers asked him for his final answer, he knew it would be better for him to stay behind. He wasn't sure what his next move would be. Maybe he'd go back to school. Get a degree. Regardless, Rafe knew it was time to call his folks on the other side of L.A. county to let them know he'd be moving back into his old room for a while. He was beyond grateful when they welcomed him with open arms.

He missed the Bakers and aspects of their routine, but he was enjoying the freedom. He'd enjoyed catching up with his dad and working on their motorcycles together, helping his step-mom around the house, and even keeping his teenage sisters out of trouble until school started in another two weeks.

He was pretty damn shocked when he got a call from Winnie Baker's teacher. She got right to the point and when Rafe agreed to at least check things out, they hung up and she texted him all the contact information he needed. It had happened so fast, he was in a daze when he stepped back into the garage.

"Rafe." His dad's head popped up on the far side of his Harley. He'd heard his dad call his name, but his brain was still caught up in the conversation he'd just had. "Close your mouth or you'll catch some flies." This time his dad's thick Boston accent caught his attention. Rafe shook his head and swallowed.

"Yeah, sorry. What'd you say?"

"Who's on the phone?"

He glanced again at the texts that had just come through. "Uh, Sarah Kato. She was Winnie's teacher last year."

"And? What did she want? You look like she just confessed to switching Winnie out for a robot."

"Nah. One of their incoming parents at Whippoorwill is having a childcare emergency. She needs a live-in by Monday. Single mom."

"She want you?"

"Well, yeah. Sarah said she recommended me."

"You gonna do it?"

"I don't know. Give me one sec."

"Yeah. Take your time."

"I'll be right back." Rafe almost took a seat on the weight bench against the back wall, but his body switched to autopilot, directing him right to his old bedroom. He'd taken personal offense when his step-mom announced her plans to turn his bedroom into a guest room, but she'd really been on to something when she switched out his shitty twin bed for a Cal king.

He sank down and grabbed his laptop off the nightstand, then googled Dr. Sloan Copeland at the ULA Medical Center like Sarah suggested. When he clicked on her profile on the ULA website, he did one hell of a double take. Dr. Sloan Copeland was hot as fuck. And young. Rafe didn't know how long it took to become a heart surgeon and even factoring in what his step-mom had explained to him about Black women and aging, Sloan Copeland looked five minutes over twenty-one.

The photo on the website was your standard professional headshot, Sloan sporting a white lab coat over blue scrubs, but she looked like a model. Her dark brown skin was practically glowing. High, round cheeks framed her plump lips, which were turned up in a bright smile that showed off perfectly white teeth. Her hair was in long braids that she'd put up in a high bun. Her looks aside, Rafe was stuck on the timeline of having two six years olds and finishing all her medical training. Not impossible, but obviously hard.

He clicked around on a few more links and some things slid into place. Article after article, including profiles in

Ebony, Essence and O Magazine about the child prodigy bound for Harvard Med School. More articles and posts on the youngest doctor to complete a surgical residency at US Medical Center in Seattle. If his internet math was correct, she was twenty-eight. Still pretty young for an established doctor.

He realized how far down the rabbit hole he'd gone when he scrolled through a good portion of her Instagram. There were plenty of pictures of her twins, and close ups of human hearts on full display. Dr. Sloan Copeland appeared to be enjoying a full life. And she needed his help with her kids. Eventually, when Rafe found himself searching through her social media looking for pictures of just Sloan on her days off, he knew he'd gone way off track. Yeah she was hot, but that wasn't a part of this equation. He walked back out to the garage.

"What are you thinking?" his dad asked as soon as he stepped back outside.

"Single mom. She's a doctor. Two girls. Nanny bailed last minute, so it looks like she could use the help."

"How old are the kids?"

"Sarah said they're six. They're twins."

"You can handle that. Two kids is a walk in the park for you."

"I know." Rafe knew his dad was right. The Bakers' four kids were actually pretty easy to handle. Before that, he'd been with the Craigs and they had five kids, and before that he'd helped his step-mom with his sisters, who were only a year apart. He could handle twins.

"So what's the problem?"

"Just what I told you. I have to move on at some point."

"Yeah, but it's not like you to leave a lady in the lurch like that."

"She needs a nanny, Dad. Not a lift from the airport."

"I know, you smart ass."

"I'm just saying. This is more of a commitment."

"How much commitment can you handle?"

Rafe didn't respond right away. Yeah, he had plans, or he was planning to have plans, but he hadn't put those plans into motion yet. He wanted to relax some more. Spend time with his sisters and parents. It had taken him two weeks to switch off and his internal clock still had him rising at six to get four kids out the door on time. He was in recovery mode, not start a new career mode.

"I can give her to the end of the year."

"There you go. Let her know up front and then she'll have plenty of time to find your replacement."

"Yeah. Yeah, I'll do that. Let me go call her."

"Bring me a water on your way back."

"A water?" Rafe asked, shocked. His dad's sophisticated thirst could usually only be quenched with Coors, black coffee or knock-off grocery store Mountain Dew, which he drank proudly if he was feeling festive. He was surprised the old man didn't glow in the dark.

His dad was suddenly interested in his tool box. "Apparently dehydration is a thing. Your mom says I have to drink more water or find a new wife."

Rafe didn't even bother to cover his laugh. "Water it is." But first he had to give Dr. Sloan Copeland a call.

Chapter Two

Sloan tried to get comfortable in the McDonald's booth, but it wasn't working. The last few days had been stressful as fuck and her nerves were fried. Drew had taken the news about Tess surprisingly well. Sloan was shocked that he didn't attribute her shady exit to something Sloan had done, but he did manage to slide in a few predictable jabs about how none of this would have happened if she'd stayed in Seattle.

That was her cue to end their call. She told him she'd be in touch when she found someone new, then "accidentally" hung up on him. As she tried to force herself to get some sleep, she reconsidered Xeni's offer. Maybe she could put a hex on Drew. She woke up the next morning with both girls in her bed. They got clingy when they were stressed out. She wanted to strangle Tess anew, but she had to move on.

She sat close to the entrance with an eye on the twisting tubes and ladders of the Play Place. She glanced at Avery talking with their sitter, Stacia, before looking back at the door. They were early. She still lived by her father's mantra: five minutes early was late. She didn't know how true that was until she had kids. She'd given herself plenty of time to get the girls ready and out the door so they would be on time to meet with Rafe Whitcomb.

Sloan had never considered hiring a male nanny, but when her friend and Xeni's fellow teacher Sarah insisted he was perfect for the job and *available*, she knew she'd be a fool not to check him out. Especially when all the other avenues she'd tried had come up empty.

Her colleagues at the medical center had a few recommendations for babysitters and she'd signed up for a childcare service, but their extensive vetting process left her in a bind for the coming weeks. She needed someone now. He'd called while she was busy with a consult, but when she found a few minutes to call him back, they'd had a pretty good talk.

He was thirty-four and had just finished working with a family who had decided to move overseas. He'd recently updated his first-aid and CPR certifications. Sloan was impressed by the thorough questions he had for her, beyond the girls' ages and food allergies. He wanted to know upfront exactly what she expected from him, her parenting style, and her day-to-day vision for how he not only fit into the girls' lives, but hers as well.

She ignored the weird tingle that line of questioning shot up her spine, just like she ignored the sexiness of his deep voice, with its hint of a Boston accent. The focus was finding a nanny for her kids, not a phone sex buddy for herself.

She also appreciated that he didn't flinch when she asked about his political leanings. No politics, no religion, no money mentions were a thing of the past. Rafe might be qualified, but she was trying to raise two young, biracial Black girls and she'd be damned if she let someone who was a fan of walls and assault rifles and playing fast and loose with general human rights spend that kind of time around them.

He explained then that at fifteen he'd been picked up on an auto theft charge and spent six months in juvenile detention camp. Prison and police reform were things he held close to his heart. Sloan hadn't expected him to come with a criminal past, but he was upfront about it, explaining that it didn't appear on his background check since he'd been a minor. It was his one and only offense, and from the details he gave her, it sounded more like an instance of a young kid trying to fit in in a new city than the backstory of a violent criminal mastermind.

By the end of their conversation, she was satisfied that Rafe seemed competent and capable. And honest. She was further impressed when Haylene Craig called her not an hour later to give Rafe a glowing recommendation. He'd watched her children before he'd been employed by the Bakers, who also emailed that evening to say that having Rafe with their family had been a wonderful experience and that they missed him terribly.

After she put the girls to bed, she called Rafe again and asked if he'd be interested in meeting them on Saturday morning to see if they all meshed well. They agreed on the McDonald's near her house and that if they could execute phase one of the in-person interview without incident, they'd move on to phase two.

Sloan had tried to stalk him on social media, but she couldn't find much. Mostly pictures of motorcycles and baked goods that he'd prepared. She was able to find a few candid pictures confirming that he was a white guy with red hair, but he clearly wasn't the type to upload a bunch of selfies.

Sloan checked her phone one more time, absently registering the sound of a motorcycle that had just pulled in the parking lot. Technically they weren't supposed to meet for another five minutes, but she was ready to get on with it. Movement at the top of the jungle gym tube caught her eye. Sure enough, Addison had managed to scale the outside. Just as she was about to hop up, Stacia was on it. Addison made a face as she shimmied backwards and back into a large hole in the green plastic.

"Dr. Copeland?"

Sloan almost dislocated her neck as she whipped her head around at the sound of a newly familiar voice. If pictures were worth a thousand words, the few pictures she'd seen of Rafe Whitcomb had left out some pretty important details. They didn't tell her that he was easily six foot five or that he was covered in tattoos from wrist to neck. They did clue her in to the motorcycle thing. She might have been staring up at his bright blue eyes, but that didn't stop her from catching a glimpse of the motorcycle helmet hanging from his long, thick fingers. Those lying ass pictures left out the part where he'd grown a perfectly thick, gloriously manicured beard.

"Yes, right. Hi!" Like a dumbass, Sloan stood too fast and realized a bit too late that she was trapped by the low table. Luckily Rafe didn't laugh at her as she squirmed out of the booth. She swallowed and smoothed down the front of her outfit before holding out her hand. "Rafe. Hi. Nice to meet you."

"Likewise." His fingers gripped hers in a firm, but brief handshake.

"The girls are just playing. I thought we could talk for a few minutes and then you can meet them."

"That sounds good." God, his voice was sex on a biscuit. "Let's sit," he said, motioning back to the booth.

"Where are you from again?"

"Woburn, Mass. Near Boston."

"Yeah, okay. I'm from Rhode Island. Providence." Sloan needed to chill. *Her* voice was doing that high floating thing it did when she was nervous. She hadn't made those wheezing, squeaky sounds since she met Drew. She was going to ignore that inconvenient fact and get right on with her day. "Your accent is making me homesick." Sloan watched Rafe as he supressed a smile. Sloan tried not to read too much into that.

"I tried to get rid of it, but I've been spending time with my dad. When I'm around him, it comes back."

And there it was. An awkward silence. Then Sloan knew, there was no mistaking it. He'd realized she was checking him out.

"So," Rafe said.

"So, right. How are you feeling about this? I know it's extremely short notice. Ideally—well, not ideally—but, I'd like you to start tomorrow if we feel like things will work out. Sunday would technically be your day off, but you can get moved in and the girls can at least have a sense of you being in the house before you're on your own on Monday."

"Why don't I meet Avery and Addison? Let them be the judge." His tone was even, but Sloan could hear what he was trying not to say. *Slow the fuck down, lady. I haven't agreed to this yet.* Sloan felt herself slipping further into the jackass hole. That was the point of them meeting today—to see if they even fit, not for her to make heart eyes at him in a semi-crowded fast food restaurant. The part of her brain that was actually inhabited by a smart, professional, self-possessed woman got her ass in gear and gestured toward the indoor playground.

"After you," he said. Sloan nodded with a tight smile, then led the way. She took a deep breath as she went. She used the fact that he wasn't checking her out to recalibrate her line of thinking. Rafe Whitcomb was drop dead gorgeous and that didn't matter one bit. She entered the play area and narrowly missed stepping on a feral toddler as it ran by.

"Hey, love bugs. Can you please come here? I have someone for you to meet."

"Is it Rafe?" Avery yelled as she emerged from the base of the slide. She took one look at him and froze.

"This is our neighbor, Stacia."

"Hi." The nineteen-year-old's eyes nearly popped out of her head as she offered a shy, little wave. *Same, kid. Same,* Sloan thought. Only Addison seemed to be completely unbothered by Rafe's hulking presence. She hopped off the jungle gym, walked right up to him and tapped his helmet.

"Do you have a motorcycle?"

"Nice to meet you. I'm Rafe," he said in response. Meanwhile, Avery was inching closer, her mouth still hanging open.

"I'm Addison and that's Avery. We don't model."

Rafe glanced at Avery, then back at her sister. "Good to know. Nice to meet you, Avery." He got nothing in response. She was still in shock, and Sloan didn't push her. The girls sometimes took turns being the bashful one. Avery would come around, especially when she felt that Addison had tested the waters enough for them both.

"Can I hold your helmet? Please?" Addison asked.

"Yes, you may. And I appreciate the please. Thank you," he said. "Here you go. Use both hands, it's heavy." Addison held up her open palms and let Rafe place the black helmet in her grasp. Sloan knew her child so well, she knew exactly what she was going to do as soon as her little nose scrunched up, but by the time she said, "Don't sniff it!" it was too late. Addison had already pressed the seam where the interior lining met the hard outer shell right into her nose.

"It smells like sunscreen. Can I wear it?"

"Maybe later."

"Okay," Addison replied, She handed his helmet back, dreams crushed.

"Thanks." Rafe looked over at Avery. "Do you want a go?" Avery stepped behind Stacia and shook her head. "Well, you let me know if you change your mind."

"So I thought Rafe could hang out with us. We'll go to Jo-Ann like I promised, and then we can go home and you can do some arts and crafts with Rafe while I get lunch ready."

"Can we go in the pool, too? I'm so hot," Addison whined.

"I don't know, baby. I forgot to tell Rafe we have a pool. I don't think he brought his swim trunks with him today."

"I did," Rafe piped in. "Got a whole just-in-case kit in my bag."

"Alright, then. Yes, we can go in the pool. Let's go," Sloan said cheerfully.

"Ladies first."

"Thank you." Sloan ushered Addison toward the door, with Avery still clinging to Stacia. As soon as they stepped outside, she spotted a shiny, like-new, black and gold sportbike gleaming in the late morning sun. After they got the girls settled in their car seats in the back of the Mercedes, Sloan turned around and nearly orgasmed at the sight of Rafe astride his Ducati. Lord, his legs were long and his thighs were thick. And he was completely off limits.

"There's a Jo-Ann's—"

"On La Cienega and Pico?"

"That's the one."

"I'll see you there. Any tricks with Avery I should know about?"

"Nah, she's just being bashful. She's the powder keg. Just give her a few hours. She'll be asking you to play the most cutthroat game of Marco Polo."

Rafe nodded, his face otherwise expressionless. He lifted his helmet, a clear cue that this portion of the conversation was over and maybe Sloan should stop staring at him. Right. She climbed in the car and turned to Stacia.

"Do you mind hanging around for a few more hours? I think Avery is scared of him."

"I'm not *scared*. I'm practicing stranger awareness," Avery declared from the backseat.

Stacia smiled. "Yeah, of course."

"Great. Ready, girls?"

"I am!" Addison yelled, before she started chanting "I love crafts! I love crafts!"

"Rafe is coming with us?" Avery asked.

Sloan looked at her daughter in the rearview mirror. "Yes, he is. Are you okay with that?"

"Yeah, I guess." After a beat, she went on. "He's taller than Daddy."

"You're right, he is," Sloan said, choosing to ignore the loud snort Stacia failed to keep to herself.

•

Rafe was fucked. He knew there was a chance that Sloan Copeland would be even hotter in person. He knew from talking to her on the phone that her sweet voice might be even more intoxicating. He was dead fucking wrong. Dr. Sloan Copeland was a fucking smoke show, a twelve out of ten stunner. He couldn't imagine what patients thought the first time they saw her approaching their hospital bed. Part of him prayed like hell that he would hate her children. Not the case.

Addison was hilarious and really in your face, but she understood her pleases and thank yous. Avery couldn't take her eyes off of him, and even as they made their way around the craft store she refused to speak to him, choosing instead to whisper her responses to Stacia. He intimidated other adults, so he wasn't shocked that a six-year-old was a little wary of this man popping up in her life. No, the kids weren't a problem at all. And Dr. Sloan Fucking Copeland was a goddamn delight. Sweet, charming, considerate, and patient as hell. Addison lost her cool twice picking out crafts and toys, and Sloan calmly got her back in check with kindness and respect.

As he climbed back on his bike and followed them to the house, he didn't even think about the way she treated him. The second he set foot in that damn McDonald's and saw the way Sloan was looking back at him, Rafe knew he needed to shut all emotion down. If he didn't, he knew he'd be asking her out instead of agreeing to take care of her children. Icy demeanor firmly in place, he turned his full focus to Avery and Addison, avoiding the way Sloan's ass looked in her floral romper.

Around the seventh time that Addison asked him if she could use his shoulders as a diving board, he knew he was going to say yes to the job. He hadn't told Sloan that he was only available to the end of the year. He'd wanted to wait and meet her first and feel out the whole situation. He was on board, but now he needed to come up with a way to watch Sloan's children while avoiding Sloan completely. He scooped Addison up one more time and gently tossed her over his shoulders into the deep end of the pool. A few feet away, Avery was showing Sloan how long she could hold her breath underwater.

Rafe looked over as Avery's head popped above the surface, her dark curls plastered to her forehead.

"Very good, baby!" Sloan cheered from her submerged perch on the pool steps. Her tits looked amazing in the simple orange one-piece she was wearing. "I counted to ten that time."

"I can get to twenty," Avery insisted as she doggy paddled over to the edge. "I want some water."

Rafe realized then that he was pretty thirsty himself. "Hey Avery, can you show me where I can get some water too?"

"I think it would be very nice of you to show Rafe where we keep the cups," Sloan said.

Avery considered her options for a moment. Then she climbed up the inset ladder, out of the pool, turning toward Rafe with her hands on her hips. "You have to follow me, but you have to dry off first. We can't track water inside."

"Deal."

Rafe swam to the edge of the pool, away from the steps where Sloan was sitting, and hoisted himself out. He grabbed his towel off the deck chair, then followed Avery inside after they were both done drying off. She marched into the brand new white on white on slate grey kitchen that was attached to an even larger open concept living and dining area. She went straight for the massive pantry.

"We keep the stool in here. It's not a toy," she said in a stern tone. She opened the door and pulled out a wooden step, dragging it over to the faux wood, clearly scratch-resistant tile. Rafe watched as she carefully made her way up each step until she could kneel on the counter. "Mommy said feet belong on the floor and we can't walk up here."

"Got it. I won't walk on the counters." Avery seemed like she had things under control, but he moved a little closer just in case. She grabbed two plastic cups from the cabinet, gently set them down on the counter, then carefully climbed back down.

"You want me to fill these up while you put your step stool away?" he asked.

"Yes. Thank you very much." Rafe kept his smile to himself as they stood in the middle of the kitchen and enjoyed their ice cold water. When Avery finished, she put her cup on the counter and looked Rafe dead in the eye.

"I can use that again with my lunch."

"Very resourceful of you."

"You're really big." She cocked her head to the side, trying to make sense of him.

"I am."

"Like, you're as tall as the house."

"I'm not sure that's right, but I am pretty tall. My dad's tall too and so was my mom."

"My mom's short."

"She's short-ish. She's about average height. Do you know what average means?"

"No. I have to pee."

"My bad. Please." Rafe moved out of the way. Avery walked backwards down the hall, keeping a firm eye on him until she disappeared around the corner. He had to appreciate her vigilance. No one was going to get the jump on Avery Copeland.

Rafe refilled his water glass. He needed a few more minutes before he laid eyes on Sloan again. He got about thirty seconds. Sloan came walking into the kitchen, Addison wrapped in a towel by her side. "I think we're ready for some lunch. What about you two—oh. We're down one."

"Water break turned into a bathroom break."

"Ah, okay," Sloan said as she absently stroked the back of Addison's head. "Are you hungry?" she asked Rafe.

"I could definitely eat." Your pussy. Right now. Splayed out on this kitchen counter.

"Great. Miss Addison, you know the post-pool drill."

Addison nodded. "Rinse off, lotion up."

"Thank you, ma'am."

Addison turned on her heels and ran for the stairs.

"How many peanut butter and jam sandwiches does it take to satisfy a man your size?" Sloan asked with a teasing smile. She wasn't flirting. It was an honest question. Instead of giving her an honest answer, he wanted to tell her what a man his size can do for her.

"Wonderbread sandwiches, five. If you have some thick artisanal slices from your local Whole Foods Market, I should be okay with two."

"Good lord, you're going to eat me right into the poor house." Sloan laughed and turned toward the fridge. "You're in luck. We have both. You have a preference?"

"Nah. Surprise me. Dealer's choice."

"Mom?" Rafe turned at the whine in Avery's voice.

"Yes, baby?"

"I'm hungry. So, so hungry. I'm sooooo hungry. Help."

"Well sister, you are also in luck. Go get washed up and lunch will be ready in a bit."

"Okay." She looked like she was going to head upstairs, but she looked dead at Rafe again. This kid was really letting him know who ran things around here. "Are you going to be our nanny this time? Our nanny quit and it was rude."

"I think your mom and I are going to talk about it. Can we let you know when we know?"

"Okay. If you're not going to stay, say goodbye first," Avery said as she grabbed the edge of the counter and started jumping up and down. "Leaving without saying goodbye is rude."

"You're right. I will not leave without saying goodbye."

"Okay." Avery hopped up and down a few more times before taking off to join her sister.

Sloan rolled her eyes. "See, she came around."

"She's tough, but fair."

"True," Sloan said with that smile that Rafe was starting to love before a sober look came over her face. She leaned against the counter, arms across her ample chest. She was ready to talk business. "So, I don't want to sound desperate, but please say yes. The girls love you and my Spidey senses are telling me that you're obviously a good guy."

"I wouldn't say all that," Rafe let slip.

"God, just tell me now if you're secretly a huge asshole."

"I—I think we have problem."

Sloan's expression dropped. "What is it?"

Rafe sucked in a deep breath and decided it was best to tell Sloan the truth. She was only growing on him and seeing her every day, even if only for a few hours, wasn't going to make things any easier. "I've never worked for a single mother I was this attracted to before. I am very attracted to you."

"Oh?" Sloan seemed genuinely confused, like he'd be a fool to think she could be anything close to sexy.

"Is that crazy?"

"Yes? I—no? I just—I didn't expect you to say that. I—nevermind. Okay." Sloan let out a long sigh, then put her hands on her hips as she examined those scratch-resistant faux wood tiles. He could see where Avery got the gesture from. "I guess it's not impossible."

"Are people not usually attracted to you?" Rafe asked. It was his turn to be confused. How was every man who encountered this woman not lining up just for a chance? What the fuck was her ex-husband's problem?

"Not the people I want, but that's not the issue. How big of a problem are we talking?"

"It's not going to impair my judgement, but I've been trying not to look at you all day."

"Oh." Rafe watched her beautiful face as her full lips twisted up at the corner. "Okay. Well. Unless you think it'll impact your ability to look after the girls… do you?"

"No," Rafe said honestly. Yeah, he wanted Sloan. Bad. But that wasn't enough to change who he was at his core. While he might be blunt and honest, he wasn't stupid and he wasn't a dick. This casual Saturday afternoon was a breeze, but Sloan needed someone she could trust to hold things down twenty-four seven.

From what she told him, she operated for hours upon hours, a few days a week. And even when patients' lives weren't in her literal hands, her job came with a lot of demands. She couldn't settle for a nanny who would do anything less than help her children thrive. He knew he was the right person for the job. "It won't be a problem."

"Okay, good. Let's see how the rest of the day goes, but I'd really like it if you could start tomorrow. I can handle your attraction to me, if you can."

"Yeah, I guess. Sounds good."

"Good." Then Sloan changed the subject like he hadn't just told her wanted to deep dick her into next week. "Can I put you on apple slices?"

"Absolutely. I'm good with a knife."

"Knife block is right there and you can grab three apples out of the crisper. Or seven. I don't know how much fiber it takes to keep this system running," she said with a little laugh as she gestured up and down his tall frame. Rafe narrowed his eyes at her and walked past her to the fridge. He grabbed three apples, rinsed them, and then settled in next to Sloan at the island and started chopping.

Chapter Three

Sloan deserved an award for her performance in "I Spent the Last Eight Hours Pretending Everything is Totally Cool." Years of telling patients that they were in the safe, capable hands of a doctor who was barely old enough to drink had kicked her people-reading skills to an eleven. She knew when people were comfortable with her. She knew when people wanted to patronize the shit out of her, but had the decency to hold their rude comments back. She also recognized a good vibe when she saw one. She could tell that she would click with someone on more than one level.

Or so she thought. All day, Rafe had been completely polite and perfectly sweet with the girls, which was all that mattered right now. With Sloan? He'd been cordial with a side of frosty. Not mean, but he was making it very clear what kind of a professional he was and how important it was to him to bond with the girls. Which was exactly what Sloan wanted and the exact reason she did the smart thing and packed up her drooling lust for Rafe in a neat little box and tucked it way in the back of her brain attic. She'd planned to leave it there to collect dust until she forgot all about it. And then Rafe had to go kick down the door and spill the contents of that box-o-lust down the stairs.

So, Rafe was attracted to her. Cool. No big deal. She thought she'd handled it well. Brought the focus back to the job at hand. People were attracted to other people all the time. People were attracted to other people they worked with all the time. So, they were attracted to *each other*, even Rafe didn't know it. It was no big deal. If Rafe decided to take the job, she would just keep the nasty, filthy thoughts that had been running through her head when she watched his wet, tattooed body glistening in the afternoon sun to herself. No big deal.

The rest of the afternoon went as well as Sloan hoped it would. She hung back as they ate lunch and let Rafe talk some more with the girls while he showed them how to use crayons with watercolors. They told him that they were starting kindergarten in a week and they were excited because they'd already met their teacher Mrs. Brown and she was very nice. They wanted their "aunt" Xeni to be their teacher, Addison explained, but her classroom was across the hall, so they'd still be able to see her. Rafe knew Mrs. Brown too, and agreed that they would enjoy being in her class.

Avery finally came all the way out of her shell and peppered Rafe with questions about his tattoos. The girls were enthralled by his explanation of how the ink goes under the skin and Sloan was very pleased when he went on to explain that they had to wait until they were done growing to get tattoos of their own.

When bedtime rolled around, Avery and Addison made it very clear that Sloan needed to step all the way aside and let Rafe handle things.

"If he's going to be our nanny, he needs to know how to do it," Avery said in the same exasperated tone she used when Sloan tried to tell her something she was already knew. Sloan put up her hands in surrender and stepped aside. Addison took pity on her mom feelings and let her pick out tonight's pajamas, but after the girls were changed and in bed, Sloan slipped outside to listen at the door. Rafe really did have everything under control and Avery was on him correcting any tiny misstep. Sloan was sure they'd heard her snort of laughter when she told Rafe that he needed a manicure.

"I've been working on my dad's motorcycle," she heard him say. "These are working man's hands."

"Working men should file their nails." Avery said. Sloan was raising some cold-blooded young ladies and she couldn't be prouder.

"If you stay, you'll have to do our hair sometimes and you'll definitely have to file your nails or they'll snag on our curls," Addison said.

"Got it. Get a nail file. I'm on it. I think it's time to say goodnight."

"Tell Mom you want to be our nanny," Addison said in a stage whisper.

"I will. Do you want goodnight hugs or goodnight high fives?" he asked, scoring himself even more points.

"High fives!" both girls said.

There was a round of giggles before she heard Rafe say, "Goodnight, tiny people." A few seconds later, Rafe squeezed his large frame through the smallest crack the doorway would allow.

"They're a tough crowd, but I think I did okay," he said.

"You did great." They were so close, Sloan was forced to ignore the smell of sunscreen on him. "You want to head down to the kitchen? I'm just going to say goodnight to them and then we can talk."

"I'll be waiting." Sloan decided it was best not to wonder if there was any innuendo in his tone. Instead, she offered him what had to have been the most awkward smile before she slid into her girls' bedroom.

"So, what do you think?" she whispered as she sat on Avery's bed. Addison jumped out of her bed and came over to join them, nudging Sloan's arms out of the way so she could sit on her lap.

"I like him," she said.

"I like him too. I like him better than Tess."

"Oh, well I guess that means a lot," Sloan said. "You loved Tess."

"Not anymore. Tess is a dickhead."

"Hey!" Sloan scolded. "We don't use language like that."

"You called her a dickhead yesterday." Shit. Avery must have heard her talking to Xeni. She had to remember the NSA agent monitoring her phone had nothing on her kids.

"And I was wrong to say that. It's okay to be sad or angry with Tess, but don't call people names. I'll try to be better about it."

"Let's stop talking about Tess," Addison said with some resolve and a pained sigh. If Sloan ever saw that dickhead again...

"I like that idea. Let's move on for good. No more Tess chat. So Rafe gets a thumbs up?"

"Yes, but we have a lot to teach him. He's a boy and he's White," Avery said.

Sloan snorted. "He is both of those things. He's nice too, yeah?"

"Yeah, he's nice. And he's more patient than Daddy," Addison added.

"Oh? How so?" Drew was a good father, but he was a little high strung. Reason number 8,578 their marriage ended.

"Daddy won't let us do *anything* ourself."

Avery sprung up in her bed. "Yeah! He doesn't. Rafe is good at teamwork. Daddy wants to do everything himself."

"Okay, okay. Let's not get into Daddy tonight. I'm going to talk to Rafe and I think there's a pretty good chance that tomorrow, he will be your new nanny." That news was met with an enthusiastic "YAY!" from both girls. Sloan couldn't explain the relief she felt. The girls had been too hung up on the move to L.A. to make a real judgement call on Tess when she first hired her, but now she was glad the girls were on board with someone new, someone Sloan was pretty confident she could trust.

"So now," she sang as she stood and swung Addison around. "I say goodnight to my darling love bugs." It took her another ten minutes to get them settled again. She had to field a few more questions about tattoos, and eventually she headed downstairs to talk to Rafe.

She found him in the kitchen, finishing up the dishes. Sloan paused just for a moment to take a mental snapshot of his ink-covered forearms as he set another plate in the dishwasher. "I can handle those," she said. Her voice sounded weird again. Bitch get a grip.

"Not a problem. I think best when I'm moving around."

"I'm the same way." Sloan pulled out a stool at the island and waited until he put the last plate in the dishwasher. She tried not to watch him too closely as he dried his hands, but those arms with those tattoos were enough to make a girl sweat a little. He pulled out the stool at the corner of the island and took a seat.

"Before we get down to it, I just wanted to apologize for what I said earlier," he said

"What—oh. Right."

"I was way out of line and that was real inappropriate. You have my word nothing like that will happen again. You are very beautiful, but this," he motioned between them. "I know it's not gonna happen."

Sloan felt a twinge of disappointment she couldn't explain, and pushed that into the corner with the other odd feelings she'd been boxing up all day. "I appreciate that and I accept your apology. But you should know that I wasn't offended. If I was, you'd definitely hear about it."

"They get their frank, no-nonsense nature from you."

Sloan laughed. "Yes."

"Good to know. I'm the same way."

"I'm seeing that." Sloan looked up and even though they had squashed this whole lust at first sight issue, she couldn't handle the way he was looking at her. Like, really looking at her. His blue eyes intensely reading every emotion that must have been playing across her face. A sudden heat crept over her skin as a tightness gripped her throat. It had been a long time since she felt this way. Over six years in fact. She cleared her throat and moved on. "So."

"So."

"We had our annual Copeland family board meeting and when we got to new business, I was informed that the members would like to offer you the position."

"Hmm," Rafe leaned back and ran his fingers through his beard. Sloan suddenly realized that she was dying to know what that beard felt like between her legs. "Please tell the board that I accept."

"Wonderful." They talked again about Rafe's pay, which he seemed pleased with. He'd hopped off the Bakers' family phone plan when they left the country and set up his own. It seemed easier to leave it that way. Sloan was offering more than what the Bakers paid, more than covering his expenses in that area.

"I like to keep the girls home on Sunday. I want to get them in the habit of knowing that it's good to take a day to do nothing. That'll be your day off unless we're traveling. Saturday too, but that will be kind of a flex day. I'll let you know in advance if I need you."

And then they got to her least favorite part of the conversation. "Their father, Drew, has visitation one weekend a month. As I mentioned, he's also in cardiothoracics. He has a private practice in Seattle. I'll share that visitation calendar with you. You'll have to take them to LAX on Friday when they get out of school. Drew arranged the recurring flight and I'll make sure you're on that email."

Rafe nodded. "Is there anything else I need to know there?" He was asking about Drew.

"No. He's fine. I couldn't justify turning down the job at Med and I have primary custody," Sloan shrugged. "That's all." Also, she really hated him.

They hammered out some final details and then it was time for Rafe to go. Sloan walked him out to the driveway to his motorcycle. For some foolish reason, it felt like the end of a really good date.

Rafe climbed on his bike. Even in the dim street light, it was a lot of sexy to handle.

"I'll be back in the morning."

"Great."

He looked at her for a long moment and Sloan knew that for however long he was with her family, this was going to be difficult. "Goodnight, Sloan," he finally said.

"Goodnight." She wanted to stand there and watch him slip on his helmet. She wanted to be close enough to feel the rumble of the engine when he started up his bike. She wanted to watch him ride off into the darkness, but this wasn't a movie and they were not an item. She offered him a little wave and a tight smile, and then she walked into the house. She had a few things to do downstairs before she climbed into her own bed. Still, she lingered just inside the front door and embraced the small shiver that rippled over her skin the moment he started his Ducati up.

•

Sloan couldn't sleep. It wasn't that late, but now that she had her childcare situation sorted, she thought she could at least try to get seven uninterrupted hours of blissful rest before Avery woke her up asking for waffles.

She sat up in her bed and turned on her T.V.. *Golden Girls* reruns seemed like the perfect remedy, but even after one of Blanche's killer punchlines, Sloan was still restless. She reached for her phone and texted Xeni.

I'm screwed.

OMG. I was waiting for you to text me,
but i didn't want to blow up your phone.
How did it go?

Really good.
He's really mellow, but not a pushover.
Not too heavy handed. He's also huge
and tatted so he'll have Avery's back in
all the parking lot fights she'll surely
start along the way.

Oh good. Nothing like a large
white boy in a parking lot fight.
Why are you screwed?
Sarah said he's amazing and you clearly
think he's a good fit.

Yeah, but...
Sloan added the emoji of the monkey covering its eyes.

What the fuck's that supposed to mean?

I think he might have a little crush on me.
I mean I know he does.

Um. Details please.

He said that he's kinda feeling me.

Would it be weird to say that
my prayers have been answered?
The goddess sent you a fine man and
someone to look after your kids all in one package.
Hold on. I have something for you.

Sloan waited for the next text from Xeni, but instead her silly friend called her on FaceTime. She answered the call and immediately died laughing at the ridiculous open mouth grin on Xeni's face. She leaned over and turned on her bedside lamp so Xeni could see her.

"Why are you calling me?"

"I need you to see my face," Xeni said before dropping that crazy grin. "Wait, shit. I have to send you something. It didn't send. Call me back as soon as you get it."

"What—" Xeni ended the call and two seconds later a video text popped up.

She thought she was seeing things when she looked at the thumbnail, but when she pressed play her eyes almost fell out of her head. It was a video of a White guy and a Black guy, both shirtless in a backyard or something, going head to head in a push up contest. The White guy was definitely Rafe. Beardless and missing the tattoo that now covered the right side of his neck, but she could tell it was him.

Whoever was counting had them at sixty push ups a piece, but they were starting to slow down. At around seventy-five, Rafe looked like he was going to tap out. At seventy-eight, he collapsed to the ground before getting to his feet. The crowd around him went wild as the other man picked up steam at the obvious ego boost and did ten more pushups. Finally, the Black guy stood and they clasped palms. A gentleman's bet.

Sloan immediately called Xeni back. "Where did you find this?"

"Girl, you gotta learn how to Instagram deep dive. His sister posted it."

"Jesus."

"You're gonna hit that, right?"

"Um, no. He's my nanny!"

"That is true, but if he's single and you're single... Who is he gonna go to. HR? You are HR!"

"No."

"Okay, so what exactly happened? What did he say?"

"He said he'd never worked for a single mother that he's been attracted to before."

"And what else?"

"That's it. I asked him if his attraction to me would make it hard for him to focus on the girls. He assured me it wouldn't and then, before he left, he apologized for mentioning it. He said he'd never mention it again."

"And you believe him?"

"I mean, yeah. He just doesn't seem the type to bullshit me like that. So he thinks I'm cute or whatever, but it ends there."

"Here's my solution. Wait a few days. He could secretly be wack as hell. Like, you can be wack and good with kids. Trust me. There are some wack dudes in elementary education who are amazing with kids."

"There are wack dudes everywhere."

"Exactly. See if he's wack. Like, give him a few weeks. You might—wait. You're attracted to him, right?"

"You're asking me that? After you sent me that video? Under different circumstances, I would let him destroy this. Just wreck it."

"Okay. Well, if, after a few weeks of catching him shirtless doing the laundry or doing some adorable shit to get Addison to stop crying, you don't want him to really bang that pussy out, I'll never suggest you get with him again. But if you find yourself thinking about bouncing on his lap, I'm going to tell you to roll up on him after the girls go to sleep or while they're up with their dad. I'm going to tell you to pop a titty out and ask him what's good."

"Has this 'pop a titty out' method worked for you before?"

"I have yet to meet a man worthy of these titties. But when I do, oh I'm popping a titty *out.*"

Sloan couldn't help but laugh. "Yeah, okay."

"But for real. You've been alone for three years. If you two are into each other, just be adults and talk about it. You can figure it out and not scar the girls forever. If it's too dicey, then yeah, don't go there. But if not…"

"We're not feeling each other. He just likes the way I look and I like the way he looks."

"Mhmm, okay."

"I'm going to bed."

"Don't sprain your wrist watching that video on repeat."

"Bitch!" The last thing Sloan heard before she ended the call was Xeni's cackle.

•

Rafe went home and did exactly what he had to do. He packed up all the stuff he wanted to bring with him to the Copelands' before giving himself an at-home, budget manicure. Then he spilled a gallon of jizz jerking off to the thought of pulling the crotch of Sloan Copeland's bathing suit to the side and fucking her clean into next week.

He'd told her how he felt and her confused reaction made it clear that even if she liked the look of him, her attraction ended right there. It made sense. This was the real world, not some perfect fantasy where he could somehow engage in a no strings attached fuck-a-thon with the single mother he now worked for.

He fell asleep with Sloan on his mind, but when he woke up in the morning, he was ready to get back to business. His job for this week was to get a sense of Avery and Addison's rhythms and to look for areas where he could be more helpful to Sloan.

Rafe rolled out of bed and walked into the kitchen where his step-mom, Monica, was making some toast.

"Good morning," she said, her voice still gravelly.

"Rough night?" Rafe kissed her on the cheek, then started digging around the fridge. He found just enough real milk for his cereal. His sisters already tore him a new one for trying out their almond milk.

"We didn't stop playing until two, but I won. And I finally got to cuss out Larry Page for disrespecting your father."

Rafe bust out laughing. Monica engaged in some pretty intense spades tournaments with her friends from her old neighborhood. His dad was terrible at the game and people loved to give him shit for it.

"I'm sure Joe appreciates you defending his honor. He could also just learn how to play."

"He said he can't play against me because he loves me too much to win and he can't be my partner because he's distracted by my beauty."

"Oh, that's slick."

"That's your daddy. Hope dragged him out on another one of their nerd adventures, so I'll drop you off at the doctor's house when you're ready."

Before he could thank her, he heard the telltale sign of a teenager sprinting across the house. Seconds later, his other sister, Gracie, came sliding into the kitchen. She was still in her night shirt and sporting a pair of Spongebob slippers.

"You got the job with the Copelands?" she said with a big smile on her face.

"Yeah, I gotta leave in an hour. Mom is dropping me off."

"Can I come with you? I really want to meet her." Rafe glanced over at Monica before turning his attention back to the amped fifteen-year-old. "What? I googled her. She's the youngest surgeon ever to perform a successful heart transplant and she's Black!"

"Let me ask her." Rafe pulled his phone out of his pocket and sent Sloan a text.

> *Morning, I hope this isn't too intrusive.*
> *My little sister googled you and*
> *she's dying to meet one of the most*
> *accomplished surgeons in the country.*
> *Is it okay if she swings by with me?*
> *My step-mom is coming too.*

Sloan sent back the laughing emoji with her reply.
I'd love to meet them both.

> *Thanks.*
> *Last time I'll show up with an entourage.*
> *I swear.*

It's fine. The girls won't stop asking
how many more minutes until you get here.

That warmed his chest. They were growing on him too.

> *Tell them very soon.*

He slipped his phone back in his pocket, then turned to Gracie who was still standing there, anxiously awaiting Sloan's response. "You can come. Put on pants though."

"Pants? I can't show up at Dr. Sloan Copeland's house in pants. I need to impress her. Only my spring formal gown will do. If you peasants will excuse me."

"Who are you calling a peasant? I'm the queen of this house," Monica replied.

"Too true. Not you, mom. Just this bum." She stuck out her tongue at him.

"You can stay here."

"No! I'll be nice, I swear."

"Yeah, yeah. Go get dressed." Gracie took off for her room. It was the smart thing to do. "She used to be cute. Remember?" Rafe said.

"I can't blame anyone but myself. She got my mouth. Let me put on my face and I'll be ready to go."

"Sounds good."

An hour later, they left his folks' place and headed toward Westwood. Gracie whistled when they pulled up to Sloan's house. "I have to study more." Rafe couldn't imagine what a new build with a pool in that area cost, but he knew it wasn't cheap.

"I'll have to tack real estate listings above her desk," Monica teased as she put the car in park. Just as Rafe climbed out, one of the twins opened the door and came out on the front steps, still in her pajamas. The way she glared at him made him almost positive that he would be dealing with Avery first. Right behind her came Sloan, sporting a loose tank top and a pair of skintight yoga pants. Rafe got one look at her and knew he was absolutely fucked.

Chapter Four

Rafe took the few moments he had to make his way from the driveway to the front door to get his shit together. He was officially on the clock and Dr. Copeland wasn't his to lust over. "Good morning," he said.

"Good morning," Sloan replied. "Avery, can you say good morning?" Instead of following her mother's suggestion, Avery looked him up and down.

"Let me see your working man's hands." Rafe held out his perfectly filed nails. Avery grabbed his fingers and turned them this way and that. Then she grunted, possibly in disgust, before a sinister grin spread out over her face. "They'd look better with pink polish."

"Oh, good lord," Sloan groaned.

"Let's make it through our first week and then I'll let you paint my nails."

"Yesss."

"This is my mom, Monica, and my sister, Gracie. This is Sloan and Avery." When she didn't correct him, he knew he'd guessed right. "I imagine Addison is around here somewhere."

Sloan held out her hand and greeted them warmly. "Twin number two is really into a puzzle right now. It's wonderful to meet you. Please come in." Rafe stood aside to let Monica and Gracie follow them inside to the kitchen, where Sloan motioned for them to have a seat at the island.

"Addison, baby. Come meet Rafe's family," she said before turning back to Monica. "Can I get you ladies anything to drink?"

"Oh, we won't be staying long," Monica said, pointing a thumb in his direction. "Just wanted to keep this one from riding across town with a duffle bag strapped to his motorcycle."

"Safety first," Rafe shrugged, before he caught a glimpse of Addison coming at him at full speed. Before she could smash into him, he dropped his duffle, leaned over and scooped her right off her feet. She made a little squeaking noise of surprise as he settled her on his hip. "Hey."

"Hi, Rafe. Hi, Rafe's family. I'm Addison and that's my sister Avery."

"Lovely to meet you both," Monica said with her usual warm smile. "Rafe told me you haven't been in Los Angeles that long."

"Just a little over a year. I finished my residency in Seattle and stayed on for another couple years, but I was given an opportunity to get more experience in robotic surgery and I couldn't pass that up. The girls' dad is back in Seattle," Sloan added like she'd been asked that question a lot. "My parents and my brother and sister are back in Rhode Island."

"Oh so it's really just you here?"

"And my twosome, yeah."

"Well, I don't know if Rafe told you that me and his dad are both over at LAX. I run guest services for Delta and Joey manages the mechanics crew. Gracie and her sister, Hope, are back over at Culver City High in two weeks."

"Oh, what year are you?" Sloan asked Gracie, who suddenly turned shy.

"I'll be a junior and Hope's gonna be a senior."

"Oh, that's fun."

"I guess."

Sloan stroked Avery's hair. "These two have their first day of kindergarten next week."

"Are you excited?" Gracie asked.

"Yes," Avery said quietly. Rafe almost laughed.

"Well, we won't tie you up any longer. I know Rafe wants to get settled in and I have to stop by the store. We don't usually get involved with Rafe's families, but make sure you get my number from him and you give me a call if you need anything."

"I appreciate that and my mom will too," Sloan replied.

"You're always our babies," Monica said as she winked at Sloan. "Let's get going—"

"Actually," Gracie chimed in. She paused, begging Monica for permission with a look. "I was hoping I could talk to Dr. Copeland about her career a little. But it doesn't have to be now!"

"Of course. Unless you're in a hurry."

Monica waved her off. "No, we're good, if we're not taking up too much of your time."

"Not at all. Here." Sloan walked over to the fridge and pulled out some sparkling water, then grabbed some glasses. Rafe knew they were really about to settle in.

"Why don't you all talk. Addison and Avery can show me where my room is again," Rafe suggested.

"Yeah!" Addison said, wiggling out of Rafe's grasp. He set her down and picked up his bag, before letting Addison drag him down the hall. "Don't worry. We know that this is your room and we have to respect your privacy."

The bedroom in the in-law suite was exactly the same as it had been the day before, but Rafe noticed a cute WELCOME sign sketched in crayon on the nightstand. "I appreciate that. Is this for me?" he asked the girls.

"Yes. I did the letters and Avery did the hearts and stars."

"Hearts and stars are my favorite. I'm so good at them," Addison said.

"I can see that. Next time we go to the craft store, I'll pick up a frame so I can hold on to this. Thank you, girls."

"You're welcome." Addison said, looking extra proud of herself. Avery was busy opening the dresser drawers.

"You can put your underwear up here," she said.

Rafe smiled, tossing his bag on the bed. "Thanks, I will."

"Is that really your mom?"

"She's my step-mom. Do you know what that means?"

"She's your other mom," Addison said.

"Exactly. My first mom passed away when I was thirteen and then when I was fifteen, my dad met Monica and they got married."

"And now she's your step-mom."

"Yes."

"She's like our grandma. Our mom's mom."

"Oh yeah?"

"Yeah. Our dad's mom is White like you."

"Interesting."

"We see White grandma on Thanksgiving and we see Black grandma on Christmas." The youngest of the Bakers was nine. Rafe had forgotten how blunt six-year-olds were.

"I'm sure they miss you all year long."

Rafe didn't have much to put away, just his clothes and a few toiletries. He'd deal with the rest after the twins went to sleep. While he filled up the dresser, he let the girls ramble on about their family. He listened carefully, asking gentle follow-up questions. By the time he was done, he could tell that they felt a little adrift. He could relate. Starting school would be good for them. They'd make friends and start building more of their own little universe outside of Sloan and her ex.

"I'm all done," he said. "Come on."

"We have to stay home today, but you can help me finish my puzzle," Addison said as they walked into the kitchen.

"I'm in. Let's do it. But first, I have to check on something." He lightly touched Sloan's elbow. She was in the middle of telling Gracie about changes in undergrad requirements. When she turned to face him, he forced himself not to be affected by her smile.

"Hey."

"Sorry to interrupt."

"Not at all. What's up?"

"The keys to the Tahoe? I just want to see how much gas is in it."

"Oh god," Gracie groaned.

"What?" Sloan asked.

"You will literally never run out of gas as long as he's living with you. He and my dad, all the time, 'You got enough gas? You need gas? Make sure you stop and get gas?' It's best not to fight it. He's gonna make sure you got gas."

"Good to know," Sloan said with a snort as she walked to other side of the kitchen where four sets of keys were hanging on hooks. She handed him a Chevy key on a ring with a few other keys.

Rafe took them with a "thank you," then shrugged. "Old habit. Top off the tank on Sunday. Nothing worse than hopping in the car Monday morning with cranky children and realizing you have to stop for gas."

"Okay, that's smart. Enjoy."

"I will." Rafe headed out to the garage and was hit by the stifling heat that was already building up in the oddly clean space. Sloan liked to keep things in order. Rafe walked around the back of Sloan's Mercedes, pressing the automatic lock on the Tahoe. He opened the driver's side door and was punched in the face by the worst fucking smell in his life. Something had died in that car and started to rot. He shook his head, then took another whiff. Definitely rotten fruit and something else. He took a quick look around, but could find anything. He was starting to sweat and even if he found the source of the foul as fuck stench, he needed to properly air the car out. He went back inside.

"Everything okay?" Sloan must have seen the look on his face.

"Yeah. There's just something rotting in the Tahoe. I'm gonna take it to get detailed."

"Oh gross. I'd say you don't have to do that, but—"

"Better him than you," Gracie said.

"Pretty much."

"It's why you pay me the big bucks. I'll bring you a receipt."

"Can we come?" Addison asked.

"Yeah! I wanna go." Avery added.

"Next trip to the car wash, yeah. I think this smell is something you'll want to skip."

Addison pouted. "But I wanna smell it."

"I'll be back. Feel free to show these two the door any time," he said, gesturing between his step-mom and Gracie.

"Boy, if you don't get lost," Monica said, shooting him that look that let him know she was still the boss.

"No, I love having you ladies here. I still feel new to L.A.. It's so nice to meet more people outside of the hospital."

"Okay, well you keep this women's bruncheon going. I'll be back." Rafe kissed Monica on the cheek and high fived his sister and the girls. He tried not to make it too weird by just offering Sloan a firm nod. Back out in the garage, he opened the garage door so he wouldn't be trapped inside that funk coffin a moment longer than he had to be. When the door was all the way up, he took a deep breath, then climbed behind the wheel.

•

Three hours and two rotten bag lunches later, Rafe pulled back into Sloan's driveway. Monica and Gracie had left about an hour before, according to the text Gracie sent him.

We bounced.

Sloan is so cool!
Marry her.

He sent back a gif of Danny DeVito shaking his head no. Gracie replied with a few laughing emojis. The smell was gone, but Rafe knew that stench would haunt his nostrils for years to come. He was exhausted after sitting outside in the pounding heat. Even under the shaded waiting area at the car wash, he'd started to sweat. Blasting the AC helped cool him down and circulate the strong new car smell coming from the air freshers, but he was still a little worn out. He took a few seconds to shift gears before walking back into the house.

"It's me," he called out. He found Sloan and the girls cuddled up together on the couch, watching *Moana*. He'd spent over a decade of Sundays coming home to find the parents and kids he worked for going about their afternoons and evenings, but something about this felt different. He knew what it was, but he decided to ignore what it meant and how ridiculous it made him sound.

"How'd it go?" she asked.

"Good. Your car smells springtime fresh."

"Did you find out what it was?"

"Two sandwiches that I think contained a type of lunch meat and two rotten oranges."

"What the—didn't I make you guys turkey sandwiches last Monday? For your trip to the beach?"

"Yeah…" Avery sounded real damn guilty.

"Tess wanted Tito's for lunch, but she told us not to tell you," Addison said.

"Did you hide your sandwiches under the seat?"

"Yeah…"

"One under the seat and one tucked up in the backseat. Center cup holders," Rafe added. It was ingenious really, how one of them had perfectly arranged the bag lunch so the orange fit in the cup hole. Finding that was an extra fun surprise.

Sloan squeezed her eyes shut and let out a deep breath. "Okay."

"Are you mad?" Addison asked.

"I am upset with Tess. Not with you. It's okay. But from now on, please don't leave any food in the car if you can remember, okay?" She glanced at Rafe like she knew it was a pipe dream, but she at least had to try.

"I will remember," Avery replied, her attention already back on the screen. Rafe made a note to check the car every night, just in case.

"Can we work on my puzzle now?" Addison asked. She was also ready to move on.

"Absolutely. Let me just go change my shirt."

"You're not technically on. You still have some time to yourself," Sloan reminded him.

"I know, but I'm also in the mood for a good puzzle."

"Okay." He was going to dream about the way her plump lips turned up at the corner. He changed quickly, then joined Addison at her little aqua blue coloring table. It took her an hour to finish the puzzle, but Rafe liked to think he offered just the right amount of guidance.

•

Their relatively easy morning melted down into one hell of an afternoon. Sloan tried to save Rafe.

"Sunday is also wash day," she explained after she instructed the girls to go get ready for their bath. "I wash and detangle their hair, and they both do their level best to murder me. I will never ask you to participate in this process."

"You sure? Two sets of hands are better than one." Rafe wasn't a pro, but he'd been an amateur stylist since he could convince Hope to sit still.

"I'm sure, and this should be your day off. I used to do it while Tess was out so she wouldn't witness three mental breakdowns and note my utter failure as a parent."

"I'm sure it's not that bad."

"Oh, you just wait. No matter how bad the screams get, don't call the cops."

That made him laugh. "I won't."

"Okay." Sloan stood and pretended to crack her neck. Rafe tried not to notice the way her tits jiggled in that top. "I'm going in. Wish me luck."

"Good luck."

"Oh, we order in on wash day. Always. I wrestle two small children. Or I cook. My sanity can't handle both. And it's your day off, so you're not cooking either."

"If only Postmates could send someone to wash their hair."

"Now you're on to something." She shot him the winky gun finger then headed upstairs.

Three hours and two temper tantrums later, Rafe had to admit that Sloan had been completely right. Addison and Avery hated having their hair washed and they wanted the whole neighborhood to know it. He tried to sit by and ignore the commotion, but a naked six-year-old came streaking down the stairs with shampoo in her eyes and hid in the pantry. Before Rafe could even process what happened, Sloan calmly came downstairs with a towel.

"Which way did she go?"

"Pantry."

There was a one-sided argument about what constitutes child abuse, but in the end the mad streaker, who turned out to be Addison, could be convinced that letting her mom wash the soap out of her eyes was better than auditioning for *Naked and Afraid* in the kitchen.

After parts one through three of the process were complete, Sloan caved and let Rafe braid Addison's hair. It didn't look as good as the style she executed on Avery's hair, but Addison took the opportunity to let them all know that at least Rafe didn't try to rip all her hair out of her head. Sloan handled the slight with a roll of her eyes, but he knew it hurt a bit.

By the time bedtime rolled around, all warring sides had waved their white flags, the girls were exhausted and they decided they loved Sloan again enough to let her put them to bed. Rafe had to commend Sloan. Four kids were a handful, but there was an advantage to having a spread in ages. Twins were something else. Twins as smart at Addison and Avery were a force of nature. Rafe definitely had his work cut out for him.

Rafe said his goodnights and then joined Sloan down in the kitchen. She handed over their library card, showed him where she kept the family tablet and gave him the password, laid out the clear rules for its use and the penalties for not following the tablet rules. Rafe readjusted the alerts on his phone to help him keep the girls on somewhat of a schedule. She gave him a rough outline for her week at the medical center and said she'd keep in touch if things changed. Rafe was fine was that. The cleaning crew came on Tuesdays. The landscaping crew and the man who cleaned the pool came on Thursdays. She'd send him reminders for that too.

"Any questions?"

"Any restriction on music?"

"I can't stand that Kidz Bop shit. They love Duke Stone, Beyonce, Ariana Grande, Little Mix. General, upbeat pop and R&B and you're good. There's this one K-pop song they cannot get enough of. Trust me, they will play it for you. I actually have a car playlist for them. I'll airdrop it to your phone."

"Okay."

"Anything else?" Rafe was sure that if he thought a bit longer he'd come up with something, but Sloan looked pretty fucking done with the day.

"Nah. I think we're good for now. Let's call it a night."

"Just what I wanted to hear. Now—" she clasped her hands in front of her chest. She'd changed into a different pair of yoga pants and a looser tee shirt after the battle royale, but her body still looked just as amazing. "I'm going to have, like, half a glass of wine and watch this horrible British dating show I'm obsessed with. You're welcome to join me."

"I think I'm going to hit the showers myself, actually. But I'll catch you in the morning before you leave."

"Okay."

"Goodnight."

"Goodnight." Rafe offered Sloan a tight smile as he tapped his knuckles on the counter. He almost made it out of the kitchen before Sloan said his name. When he turned back around he knew immediately that something was up. He knew the subtle change when exhausted adults found themselves in the glorious silence of a child-free room, but the look in Sloan's eyes was filled with something else. Something more.

Or maybe that was just what he wished. That whatever this shift between them was, it was more than just two adults stealing a moment to speak as adults. But Rafe had already fucked up and said what he'd been thinking. Even though he wanted to cross the room and spread her out on the counter, make her forget all about the long day she'd had, he knew that would never happen. His dreams of a making Sloan scream with pleasure were between him and his hand.

"Yeah?"

She started to move toward him, but stopped halfway down the island. She suddenly wouldn't look him in the eye and was very interested in the edge of pristine granite. "Um, about that thing yesterday."

"What thing?"

"What you said, about me—"

"Yeah. Uh...what about it?"

"I...have never had anyone that *I'm* attracted to look after the girls."

Rafe opened his mouth to respond and then closed it. That was the last thing he'd expected her to say. His brain scrambled to catch up. He had to have heard her wrong. "Just to be clear. You are saying that we are attracted to each other."

Sloan hesitated for a long moment before slowly turning her head to the side and then nodding in an even slower motion. "Yes…"

"Okay, well—"

"But! I was thinking that that doesn't mean we need to do anything hasty. Right?"

"Right?" Rafe was so fucking confused.

"I mean, this weekend was all fun and pool parties and car washes. You haven't seen me after I've been at the hospital for twenty hours. I can be unpleasant. And what if I find out you've got one of those mud flap girls tattooed on you somewhere," she said as she looked at his arm.

"I promise you I don't."

"Well, I think we can just let that mutual attraction be what it is. And then we just see."

"We just see?"

"Yeah. Let's see if we even actually like each other. As friends."

"What changed your mind? You seemed...I don't know. You didn't seem like you were entertaining even the idea of us being friends. For good reason," he tacked on. "Someone needs to think about the children. I just didn't expect this. What changed?"

"I had a...I did some thinking. I may have phoned a friend. And I can see now that this is an unusual situation. I could pretend that we can just do our thing during the day and have no-strings-attached sex any time we found ourselves alone." Okay, that really caught him off guard. It was a miracle he kept his cool. His dick, on the other hand, woke right the fuck up. He swallowed and blinked at the same time, forcing himself to follow Sloan's line of thinking as she went on.

"But I'm just not that girl. Not that there's anything wrong with being that girl," she said waving her hands to clarify. "I just—I like things—I just need a little more time. To be ready. For...I'm not sure what."

"That makes complete sense."

"And we just met."

"That's true."

"Oh my god, this is so backwards. I'm saying I trust you with my kids, but I don't trust you with me." Rafe laughed as Sloan blew out a breath and crossed her eyes at the same time.

"Well, we don't need to make this a whole thing. We can just play it by ear. And maybe make each other a deal."

"A deal?"

"Yeah. If you're not feeling comfortable, you tell me and if I'm not feeling comfortable, I'll tell you."

"Yeah, okay. That sounds like a good deal."

"And we don't have to keep having awkward conversations about it."

"God," Sloan chuckled. "This is awkward as fuck."

Fuck it, Rafe thought. He took the leap. "How about this. When you want it, when you want more from me, just send me a simple text. Pick a—a nonsexual emoji."

"Aren't they all sexual if you put your mind to it?"

"That is true."

"I'll do some research. Come up with something original."

"Good. You and I get to know each other better and if you want this to turn into something else—"

"Just send you a text. It's that easy?"

"I don't see why it has to be any harder."

"Right. Okay. Cool. That's good. Good. Should we shake on it?" Sloan said, her throat visibly working to swallow her nerves. Rafe looked her face up and down, then made a decision that would change everything between them. He crossed the kitchen, then bent, lightly cupping Sloan's cheeks. Before their lips could meet, he felt her lean up on her tiptoes. She kissed him, wrapping her soft fingers around his wrists, keeping him in place.

Knowing they were once again on the same page, and maybe feeling like he had a little something to prove, Rafe deepened the kiss, pressing even closer and parting his lips. Her tongue eased out and brushed against his. Absolutely fucked. He knew he wasn't coming back from this, but he also knew when she eventually had to fire him because they couldn't keep their hands off each other, he would still never regret this kiss.

When he felt a groan brewing deep inside his chest, he pulled away. They stared at each other for a few long moments, breathing heavily. Rafe knew what could happen next, but he also knew at that very moment that it would be a mistake.

"Well. That was very informative," Sloan said, sounding a little breathless.

"Yeah?"

"Yeah, that'll—that'll really give me something to think about." Suddenly, she seemed to snap out of the trance they'd both been under. She winced, scratching her forehead. "In a hypocritical twist, please don't ask my kids to keep secrets from me. I'm fine if you treat them to lunch or the spontaneous trip for yogurt. But Tess telling them to keep the Tito's thing from me. I just—"

"I get it. And I won't. That's not my style. I'll have them surprise you with breakfast in bed just to keep things fresh, but you're their home base. No matter how much they like me, it's not my job to mess with your relationship with them. And clearly they don't know how to feel about lying to you either. I mean, those sandwiches were buried deep."

"Thank you."

"You okay, otherwise?"

"Yeah. It's just been a long week. I'd like the Tess-related revelations to stop."

"Listen, it's my job to make things easier for you. Not harder."

"I appreciate that. I—uh. I'm going shut things down and head up to my room. I'm going to watch bad British T.V. in my bed."

"Goodnight, Sloan."

"Goodnight, Rafe."

He turned and left the kitchen before anything else could be done or said. It was barely nine o'clock when he climbed in the shower. He knew he had a long night of trying not to beat off while silently praying for a text.

Chapter Five

Sloan waited until she heard Rafe's bedroom door close before she took off at a full sprint up the stairs. She was careful not to slam her own door, but as soon as it clicked shut behind her, she threw herself on the bed and screamed the girliest, squealiest scream she could manage right into her pillow. She'd just kissed Rafe. Rafe kissed her and it was goooood. Her body was hot all over. Just one kiss and her breasts and pussy were aching.

From the moment he'd arrived that morning, Sloan knew she was in trouble. Watching him walk up to her front door was like watching the opening scenes of a porno with a semblance of a plot. Snug dark green t-shirt stretching over his large biceps. Jeans that were somehow loose, but perfectly close-fitting at the same time, hugging his large thighs. The only thing that stopped her from drooling or asking him flat out if he wanted to use her as a finger puppet was the fact that they definitely weren't alone.

Sloan knew she had to step back and evaluate what going literal years without sex did to her brain. The sudden wave of lust that had washed over her when he offered to take the Tahoe to get washed was absurd. Thanks to her experience with her ex, sometimes her standards felt so low the bar was literally under the floor, but a short forty-eight hours with Rafe had opened this strange world of possibilities. There was a hot, sweet guy out there who was great with her kids?

How could she not find that attractive? She'd spent her whole life under someone's watchful eye. First her mother's, who wanted the best for her, and then Drew's, who wanted her to do the best for him. Xeni was right. The was no harm in telling Rafe that she thought he was cute. If things went to hell, she knew he wouldn't leave her high and dry. Worst case scenario, they had a few awkward weeks while she found someone new. If things went well…

She sat up, cutting off that line of thinking. No. Whatever was going on between them couldn't become anything *more*. This was phase one of one. Smooching and maybe a few covert trips to third base. That was it. The last time she'd wanted more, she ended up married to the asshole of the century who tried to mindfuck her out of her career. All she wanted was to look at Rafe, touch his biceps a little, and hopefully he could remind her what it felt like to have an orgasm that wasn't self induced.

In the next few days, she would be opening another human being's chest and literally cutting into their heart. She could handle that, but she was losing her mind over a kiss. She picked up her phone and texted Xeni.

Uh we just kissed.

Sloan's phone screen immediately flashed to black with an incoming call from her friend. Sloan hit ACCEPT just as quickly.

"Hey."

"I'm sorry. You type too slow and this is too damn important. Tell me everything right now."

"Well, after wanting to jump him all day long, I cracked and told him he wasn't alone in his attraction to me. We agreed to play it by ear and then he decided to seal the deal with one hell of a kiss."

"Oh, so it was good," Xeni said with a sigh of relief. "Thank god. A guy that fine being a bad kisser would have been criminally unjust."

"It would have made things a lot easier for me. He put the ball in my court and now I have to decide if I want this to stop at kissing or—"

"If you want him to break that back."

"Yep."

"I think we both know what's going to happen here."

"Do we?"

"You're gonna try to hold off and then after like a week you're gonna go mad with lust and throw yourself at him. Trust me. Once the pussy's been activated and the juices start seeping into your brain, all reason goes right out the window."

"You're wrong."

"You're thinking about fucking him right now!"

"You're wrong! Oh! I met his mom and his sister today. His step-mom. She's Black. They were both super nice."

"That's great!"

It was almost hilarious that Rafe thought she might be put out by Gracie and Monica's visit. Seeing the three of them interact with their gentle teasing only made him more appealing. And it made her feel better about hiring him. She'd spent most of the time telling Gracie about her unique undergrad experience. Before they left, Monica insisted that she was serious when she told Sloan not to be a stranger. They had only spent a short time together, but for the first time since she'd moved to L.A., her home felt full in a way that reminded her of being in her own mother's home.

"Yeah, I don't know. It made me miss my mom some. I should probably call her."

"I'm sure Pauletta would like that," Xeni said, her tone softening a bit. Thankfully she changed the subject. "So you kissed. You met his mom. I assume he's still good with the girls?"

"He's great with the girls."

"So, when's the wedding?"

"Hey, so listen. I gotta go. Early day tomorrow and all."

"Yeah, yeah. I just wanna go on record as saying I told you so."

"You told me what?"

"Oh, you'll see. Have fun saving lives."

"Bye."

•

An hour later and Sloan was still buzzing from that kiss. Watching *Match Made In Paradise* was not helping. Twelve attractive singles making out and binge drinking on an sprawling estate on the coast of Ibiza while competing for fifty thousand pounds only made her think more about having oddly intense hookups with a guy she'd just met. When Poppy and Jack got voted to spend a night alone in the Lovers' Suite and the camera captured a steamy thirty seconds of them clearly having sex under the sheets, Sloan snapped. She picked up her phone and sent Rafe a text.

Are you still awake?

After the little DELIVERED notification popped up, she immediately wished she could take it back. What the hell was she thinking? Just as she geared up to give herself the berating of a lifetime, a text from Rafe popped up on her phone.

You just sent me a U Up? text.
I just want to be clear about that.

It made sense that Sloan was terrible at this. Her first crush had been her table mate in AP bio. She was ten years old and her mother sat right behind them the whole semester. When Sloan had gotten up the courage to write him a note, he just smiled at her. Later in the week, her mom explained that a boy his age was just too old for her and the next time she walked into AP bio, she had a new table mate. Clearly she learned nothing from that interaction.

"Right. Just end this right now," she told herself as she started texting him back.

So I did.
I'm going to climb in a hole now
Goodnight to you, sir.

Sloan tossed her phone across the bed, picked up her remote and pressed the rewind button. Poppy was telling the girls about her night in the Lovers' Suite. Sloan had missed everything she said. They'd moved on to Jack doing a little bragging of his own when Sloan felt her phone vibrate on the bed. She could leave it, check Rafe's response in the morning and apologize for bothering him, but the whole universe knew she was too weak for all that. Flopping on her back, she reached for her phone and held it above her face.

Not so fast.
What are you doing?

> *I'm watching that dating*
> *show I mentioned.*

How's that going?

> *Good. One of the couples just had*
> *grainy black and white sex on screen.*
> *It was thrilling.*
> *Are you settled in okay?*

I am. Bed's comfortable
And the water pressure in the shower is excellent.

Sloan groaned out loud just thinking of a naked Rafe, hot water running over every inch of his body. She knew she should wish him a goodnight—for the third time—and stop with this high school level attempt at flirting via text, but she didn't want the conversation to end.

I'm having trouble coming up with an emoji.
This is a lot of pressure.

Come down to my room.

Aren't we supposed to drag this out?
Let the tension drive us to the point
where we can't stand it anymore
and we just rip each other's clothes off?

Is that what you want?

"I don't freaking know," Sloan said to herself. She moved to the edge of her bed and stared at her phone. Rafe was sweet and kind, and damn sexy. He also wasn't the kind of asshole who was going to make up her mind for her. She thought about Drew and the girls, and tears stung the back of her eyes. She waited a minute or so, but Rafe didn't text again. He didn't push. He'd asked her a question and he was waiting for her to respond.

I want you to make this easy on me, she typed. It was the truth. A layer of truth she didn't want to get into tonight. She wasn't ashamed of her lack of experience, but she couldn't help how it colored the way she practically avoided men since her divorce. How could she tell him that, though? She knew it was impossible for him to read her mind or even to guess what layers she wanted him to chip away at first. That wasn't going to happen, so she hit send on the text.

Come on down here
and we'll see what we can do

to make things easier.

"Okay. This is silly." Sloan set her phone down and walked into her bathroom. She checked herself in the mirror and decided it was a little too soon for Rafe to see her with her braids wrapped in her loc sock. Her pajamas were nothing fancy, but she had to admit that she looked cute in the tank top and shorts. With a deep breath, she slipped out of her room and crept down the hall, lit here and there by the ankle-height nightlights that Avery insisted she put in every available outlet. She didn't dare check in on the girls. It would be just her luck that she would wake one of them up and they would follow her downstairs.

She'd been in her own kitchen in the dark of night dozens of times, but for the first time ever she felt like she was doing something bad. God, she'd missed out on a lot. She almost thought about turning on the light in the hallway to Rafe's room, but the nightlights framing his door led the way just fine. Another deep breath and she knocked once. When Rafe opened the door in nothing but a pair of sweatpants, Sloan almost swallowed her tongue.

Her gaze traveled up and down his whole body. They'd spent the last two days together and she'd already seen him with his shirt off. She'd had plenty of time to get used to the tattoos that ran all the way up to his neck. And his muscles. Sweet Jesus, he was ripped. She'd taken it all in in the bright summer sun the day before. Watching him fill the doorway, the light from the TV at his back and the glow from the nightlights casting his features in an eerily sexy shadow, Sloan felt like she was taking him in for the first time.

"Hey," he said with that perfectly deep voice in a near whisper.

"Hey."

He stepped into the hall and right into Sloan's personal space. She swallowed as his hand came up and rested lightly on her shoulder. It shouldn't have felt so right, so easy when his fingers started caressing her skin.

"What's wrong?" he asked.

"I guess I should just tell you. Since you live in my house now and you'll probably get to know me very well."

Rafe shrugged, nodding in agreement. "That does tend to happen when you live under the same roof. Lay it on me."

"I've only been with one person before," Sloan admitted.

"Your ex-husband."

"Yeah, but I don't mean I've only had wild, penetrative sex with one person before. I mean I've only been with one person. First kiss, first time, first everything. One person. Only one person. I'm an excellent surgeon. Pretty great mom, but my confidence in the men department is pretty ehhh..."

"Do you want to talk about it?"

"Absolutely not," Sloan said, shaking her head.

"But you want to do something about it."

"Yes. If you still want to, that is."

"Oh, I want to. Come in."

Sloan stepped inside Rafe's bedroom and turned to watch him as he closed the door. A small voice in the back of her head finally told her to just relax. She wanted this. She wanted Rafe. Even though she knew it was a terrible idea, something about it felt inevitable. Her eyes traveled down to his hips as he grabbed his phone off the foot of the bed.

"How long do we have?" he asked.

"Forty minutes?"

"I'll set an alarm. It's the responsible thing to do."

"It really is."

"There. You want to sit?"

"Yeah. What are you watching?" The T.V. was paused and two men on the screen were talking in the middle of a desert.

"This show about a drug cartel."

"Is it violent? I don't do violence. It makes me squeamish."

Rafe grabbed the remote and went back out to the menu of the streaming service that was linked up to every T.V. in the house. Sloan had been sure to delete Tess's profile and add one for Rafe. "What was that show you were watching? *Match Made in Paradise*?"

"Yeah," Sloan said as she perched on the edge of the mattress. "I'm on season three, episode four."

"Let's do it. Excuse me." Rafe stood directly in front of her and held out his hand.

"Oh, sorry." Sloan stood, confused about what exactly was going on until Rafe took a seat on the bed. She almost jumped when his hand came down on her waist, but she didn't hesitate when he guided her down so she was sitting between his legs. The heat from his body surrounded her, sending goosebumps over every inch of her body. It took a few moments for her to remember how to breathe, but by the time she figured out the simple mechanics of in and out, he'd pressed play on the next episode. As the host, Emry, explained the premise of the show over the title cards, Rafe's arms wrapped around her.

"So, what's the appeal of this show?" he said in her ear.

"It's mindless, I guess," Sloan replied. Her voice had that funny lift to it again. "They literally just sit around and talk, and drink, and make out, and sometimes they do these challenges which just lead to more making out. They go on 'dates,' but really they just walk four feet outside of the villa and have a picnic."

"Ah, okay. Do you have a favorite couple?" Rafe asked.

"I like—" Rafe's hand started to move across her stomach. She swallowed the tension rising in her throat and gave the whole speaking thing another try. "I like Poppy and Jack. I think they're going to win the prize money, but Sadie and Max are my favorite."

"Interesting. By the way," Rafe's lips pressed against her shoulder and it took everything in her not to moan. "You've kissed two people now."

"You're right. I have. I didn't forget, I just—"

"I understand. I just need to leave a stronger impression. I'll stop talking now so you can enjoy your show." Sloan's eyes snapped open. She didn't realize she'd closed them the moment his mouth touched her skin. She tried to focus on the argument Sophia and Clara were having over whether or not Sophia was flirting with Paul during the last cocktail party, but all of her senses were preoccupied with the feeling of Rafe's fingers slipping under the hem of her tank top. His fingers ghosted high over her skin, higher, cupping the underside of her breast and over her nipple.

Sloan gave up trying to watch the sexy singles in action and let her head fall back. Rafe's lips continued moving over her skin, hitting that certain spot where her neck and shoulder met. He sucked on that spot, nipped it lightly with his teeth and Sloan moaned. In the back of her mind, she remembered the one time Drew had accidentally found that spot and how quickly he'd moved on. He never tried to find it again. As if he knew her mind was wandering to a bad place, Rafe's other hand slid between her legs. She was already wet, but a fresh wave of arousal made her clit ache as he moved the fabric from her underwear and her shorts around in slow circles.

Rafe scooted closer to the end of the bed, impossibly close to Sloan. She could feel every inch of him, thick and hard, pressing up against her ass. She wanted more, she wanted to touch him. She turned her head to kiss him, but their lips only met for a moment before Rafe pulled back a bit. His hands were still in place, one between her legs and the other over her breast, but for a moment they both stopped and just looked at each other.

"I want to kiss you again," Sloan breathed. Rafe didn't reply at first, and she watched as the corner of his mouth tipped up in the sexiest smile she'd ever seen. He slowly released her and moved on the bed so she was no longer between his legs. Disappointment flooded through her in the few seconds it took for him to move closer again. She let him guide her down to the bed, so she was laying across the foot of the mattress on her back. He loomed over her, those blue eyes catching the light from the T.V. as he slid his hand down her stomach and back between her legs.

"Then you should be kissing me," Rafe said. All on its own, Sloan's hand found its way into Rafe's thick red hair and pulled him down to her. Sloan wanted him so bad. Both of their mouths parted and their tongues slid together in the most delicious way.

Rafe had to know how good of a kisser he was. He had to know how good he was making her feel. Between her legs, his magical fingers pushed the layers of her clothing aside. She was soaking, dripping wet as he parted her slit. He teased her, drawing his fingers all around her pussy, around her clit, but never pushing inside the way she wanted him to. They went on kissing, his hard-on pressed against her hip, his fingers exploring, exploring, never finding their proper destination.

Finally, when she couldn't stand it anymore, Sloan took matters into her own hands, so to speak. She reached down, covering Rafe's fingers with her own and guided him to her opening. He held back though, not pushing inside. Instead, he broke their kiss and looked down at her.

"Not moving fast enough, huh?" he teased.

"No, I just want you," she said truthfully.

"And we are on a time limit. Let me give you what you want." His lips were on hers again and then he gave her exactly what she wanted. Two long, thick fingers filling her up. She knew there wasn't enough time and, even with floors and closed doors between them and her kids, enough privacy for him to give her everything she wanted. Still, with the way he worked his hand, deftly moving in and out, grinding the palm against her clit, she knew this was just a preview of what he could do to her. She'd have to make time for him to show her.

Sloan came, hard, gripping onto Rafe's wrist as a forceful tremor raised her hips off the bed. A stream of "Oh shit"s and "Oh fuck"s coming from her mouth. In the distance, Sloan could hear one of the contestants reading off a text they'd just received from the producers. A new boy was entering the villa.

Chapter Six

"You can't ask me to make such an important decision and then rush me."

"It's easy," Avery said. "Just pick your favorite animal."

"Did you pick your favorite animal?"

"No, but I picked the best animal for me to be. Now you have to pick."

"I'm going to pick, but you should know, with all this pressure, this isn't my best and final answer."

Avery cocked her head and batted her eyelashes. "You never know until you try."

Rafe was nearing the end of his fourth day flying solo with the girls and he'd already learned a lot. Like Addison was very thoughtful and introspective, except for a good two hours of the day where she turned into a pure ball of energy who really liked to run into solid objects, like Rafe and the couch. She also really liked smelling things, which made sense to him.

He always tried to remember that kids were experiencing so many things for the first time, like what the inside of his motorcycle boot smelled like. He imagined this would become a very interesting party trick when she started school in a few days. They were both pretty fucking smart, ahead of most of the six year olds he watched over in the past, with the exception of Hope, who was clearly the most intelligent member of his family.

Avery was louder, but hilarious enough to offset her volume. She was also either the most clever child he'd ever met or a bit of a sadist. Time would tell.

"A bald eagle."

"Why?"

"They can fly. They are very smart. They take good care of their young." He reached out and tickled the side of Avery's neck. She dropped the mischievous look and let out a genuine giggle. "And they look really silly when they are trying to walk across ice."

"Really?"

"I wanna see," Addison said.

"Let me just finish my masterpiece." The braids Sloan had put in Avery's hair the other day were still in pretty good shape. The style Rafe had attempted on Addison's hair looked fucking terrible though, and he owed it to her and both of their self esteems to fix it. After bringing down two different combs, four different hair products and the spray bottle they kept in the bathroom, he pulled their little blue coloring table over to the couch and got to work. He looked at the paused YouTube tutorial one more time. His parts were the issue. He had to get better at making clean parts. He looked down at Addison's soft curls and realized Avery's patience wouldn't hold out that long.

Distractions seemed to be the theme of the week for everyone under the Copeland roof. Rafe couldn't stop thinking about the way things had unfolded between him and Sloan a few nights ago. Kissing her, touching her, making her come had been fucking amazing. He'd jerked off in the shower after they kissed the first time. When she came to his room, his dick was more than ready for a second round, but the alarm he'd set had gone off before he'd sated his desire to find out how good his dick felt inside her pussy.

All he wanted was for Sloan to spend the night in his bed, even though he knew there was no chance in hell of that happening. They were just testing the waters and those baby steps didn't involve an overnight in each others' arms. She'd done the right thing and slipped out his room and back upstairs, so she could get some sleep. Rafe had jerked off again.

He knew that for as long as he worked for Sloan there was a pretty good chance he'd be building up his forearm strength. What he didn't expect was the stiff hello he'd received the next morning when Sloan was heading out. Not that he expected her to give him a four-limbed greeting in the early morning light. But he didn't expect her to go out of her way to avoid his gaze as she got her stuff together. In the short time they'd known each other, she'd been sweet, a little awkward, and warm with him.

That morning, it was clear she'd constructed a bit of a wall between them. She wasn't cold exactly, though something was definitely off. When she returned from the hospital, it was more of the same. She was oddly distant, even though Rafe had already put the girls to sleep. He understood that post-nut clarity, the logic your brain magically reclaimed when you got an orgasm out of the way and regained your sanity. He just wasn't sure how it would impact Sloan.

After running every second they'd spent together through his head, Rafe had to admit that they just didn't know each other very well. Definitely not well enough for him to know how Sloan dealt with morning afters, even when he thought they were on the same page. They also weren't in a relationship. And on top of all that, she was a fucking surgeon.

Rafe couldn't imagine the stress, the pressure that came with a job that intense. Still, instead of moving forward he felt like things had stalled out. Rafe couldn't say it didn't bother him, but there was nothing he could do about it. Good thing he had two small children he was now responsible for. Keeping children alive—an excellent way to keep your mind off your bizarre personal life.

"Grab the tablet," he told Avery, "and I'll walk you through it."

"Kick. Ass." she said, throwing her foot in the air.

"Hey, take it easy with the colorful language."

"Sorry. Kick butt, kick butt, kick butt," she sang as she danced across the room. The house phone rang just as she reached the tablet where it was plugged in. She changed course and sprinted for the kitchen.

"It's grandma!"

"That's some amazing caller ID you got there."

"Grandmas are the only ones who call the house phone," Addison explained.

"Oh, okay. If it's not your grandmother, give me the phone, please."

"Hi grandma," Avery said, nice and loud, letting Rafe know she had the situation under control. "It's Avery. I'm good. How are you?" Avery at least knew how to respect her ultra elders. "Mommy is still at work and we have to get ready for bed soon. We have new nanny. He's a boy."

Rafe glanced over at Avery, who wasn't paying him a lick of attention now. She was tracing the tile pattern with her socked feet. "Almost one week.—Okay." Avery came back over to the couch and held out the cordless phone. "Here, talk to grandma."

"Hello," Rafe said in his most polite voice. He tied off the final braid and gave Addison's shoulder a little squeeze. She looked over her shoulder, then ran toward the bathroom to check his handiwork when he gave her the thumbs up.

"So you're Rafe."

"I am. I'm not sure which grandmother I'm speaking to, but it's a pleasure to meet you."

"I'm Sloan's mom. Pauletta." Just then, he heard the door to the garage open.

"Would you like me to call you Pauletta or Mrs. Copeland?"

"Pauletta would be just fine. Thank you for asking. Where are your people from, Rafe? I think I hear a little North on I-95 in your voice," she asked as Sloan came walking into the kitchen. She never stopped being gorgeous. Still, she looked like she'd been put through the ringer.

"Right outside of Boston. Woburn." Pauletta said something about having family in Barnstable, but Rafe wasn't paying attention. He was too focused on Sloan. Their eyes met for a moment as she put her stuff down on the counter before she looked away. It had been that way all week.

"Hey, love bugs."

"Mommy!" Avery said, jumping up and down.

"It's your mom," Rafe mouthed when she dared a glance at him again.

"Oh, thanks," Sloan replied.

"Your daughter just walked in the door," he told Pauletta.

"Let me speak to her."

Rafe handed over the phone and watched Sloan's expression as she greeted her mother while simultaneously hugging Avery to her side. It took him a half second to realize that there was nothing he could do or say to check in with her at the moment, especially in front of the kids. He turned back to the living room and started cleaning up the hair supplies.

"Can you put away your toys, please?" he asked Addison as she came skipping back from the bathroom.

"Yes, I can."

"I just got in and it's almost the girls' bedtime. Can I call you back?—oh hold on. Addison, come talk to grandma. You can take the phone up to your room."

"I'll come say goodnight," Rafe added. It usually helped moved the them along if they knew everyone was heading upstairs. Sloan turned and followed the girls up. Rafe gave them a while to get their bedtime routine going, finishing his cleaning and putting all the girls' hair products back in the their bathroom. When he finally went to their bedroom, all three of them were piled in Addison's bed. Sloan was trying to read them a story, but Addison was questioning why the young girl in the book was going camping in the woods if that's where animals live.

"We live inside and they live in the woods. If people go stay in the woods, then bears should be able to come stay in our house. It isn't fair."

"I suppose it isn't fair. But I think a bear might have a hard time getting used to sleeping in your small bed. Bears are pretty big."

"Rafe is big. Why can't a bear sleep in Rafe's bed?"

"Then where would I sleep?" Rafe asked as he came into the room and sat on the edge of Avery's bed.

"With the bear!" Avery said.

"No way, girlie," Rafe said, deadpan.

The girls burst into a fit of giggles. Rafe's serious side was hilarious when it had nothing to do with them. Avery hopped off Sloan's lap and climbed under her own sheets behind him. Rafe looked down as she started lightly tugging on his arm hair. Kids were so weird.

"Should we finish the story?" Sloan asked, trying to salvage bedtime.

Addison let out a sigh then burrowed further down into her sheets, making it clear that she was pretty fucking over it. "Yeah, I guess." Sloan finished the last few pages and after they both fielded ten more questions about which wild animals could sleep inside the house—the final answer was none—Sloan seemed to relax, laughing with the girls and tickling and kissing them both before they said their goodnights. She even smiled at Rafe when he promised the girls that they could watch bald eagle videos over breakfast, but the moment they stepped back out in the hallway, she turned off again.

"Um, I have to call my mother back."

"Okay," was all he could say. He got it then. Whatever had happened between them was a one-off. No big deal. It happened. Maybe she'd realized it was better if they kept things strictly professional between them. Maybe he had been too much for her, in a bad way. Maybe she just didn't want to be bothered with him. Maybe she simply wasn't into it. It didn't change the way Rafe felt. Not in that moment. Still, he would handle it. They gave it a try and now it was over. He'd get over whatever was drawing him to her, in time. He just had stop himself from looking at her for the rest of his life.

They both stood in the hallway, not saying a word. Rafe finally took the hint and went back downstairs. His bed and more episodes of *Cartel* were waiting for him. For some reason though, he went right to the couch and turned on the Dodgers game. Almost an hour later, Sloan came lumbering down the stairs. She'd changed into another set of cute-as-fuck pajamas, with tiny-ass pink and white polka dot shorts and a matching tiny-as-fuck tank top.

"I'm starving," she said, setting the phone on its cradle. Rafe wasn't actually sure if she was talking to him. He hopped up anyway.

"I made chicken enchiladas. You want me to heat some up for you?"

"Actually, yeah. That would be great." She still wasn't looking at him, but at least she was talking to him. That was something. And just like that, Rafe realized how desperate he was for Sloan to just pay him some attention. So completely fucked.

"Here, have a seat." Rafe pulled out a stool from under the counter, then dug the plastic container full of leftovers out of the fridge. He put two enchiladas in the fancy toaster oven and poured Sloan a small glass of water. He got her attention then as he slid it across the island. She caught it before it went flying off the far end.

"Nice grab. What's troubling you, stranger?"

Sloan finally smiled, a real smile, then took a deep sip. "You're..." she started.

"I'm what?"

"Nothing." And finally she looked him straight in the eye. "I'm being unfair."

"Care to clue me in?"

"I just thought you'd lost interest, but I mean, you've been doing your job. I've been working. This must be—" she cut herself off, changing directions. "How are you not crawling out of your skin?"

"I have no idea what you're talking about."

"The other night was amazing and I've been completely freaking out. Obsessing over whether I should text you. Ask if you enjoyed yourself, if you were annoyed that I didn't get you off. But you're just walking around, cool as hell. How do you do that?"

Again, there had been a massive miscommunication. He wanted to touch Sloan every time he was near her, but they were miles away from that kind of casual ease. And then he remembered what she'd said. She wanted him to make this easy for her. He moved closer and lightly brushed the side of her neck. Her eyes closed and she leaned into his touch. Fuck, she was really exhausted.

"Okay. Let's nail this out, once and for all. I'm not a— what's the right word here? I'm a tall White dude with a bunch of tattoos. I know how that freaks people out. I've also spent my whole life being calm and gentle with children. It's alright just to *be* a calm and gentle guy."

"I'm seeing that."

"I want to make this easy for you, but I don't want to scare you away, so I'm not going to run up on you every time I see you or every time we're alone. I thought you were avoiding me. And I thought you were going to text me. What happened to that?"

"I was kind of avoiding you. And as far as the texting goes...I chickened out. I don't know. Maybe this was a bad idea. I am not casual."

"Okay. Let's forget about texts and pretending we're not attracted to each other until one of us cracks. I like you, Sloan. Period. I'm calm and I'm gentle and I'm not about the bullshit. I'm also not looking for some reason to not like you."

"It'll take, like, eight years for that to sink in." Sloan slid off the stool and faced him. At her full height, she still only came up to his chest. "I like you too. It hasn't been a whole week and I like coming home to you. I thought if I pretended you weren't taking up so much space in the room, I would somehow stop wanting you."

"Did you get a chance to talk to your mom?"

"Yeah." Another sigh. Maybe Rafe shouldn't have brought Pauletta up. "We talked about Tess, actually. Every time there's a change in my life, my mom gets anxious. In a nutshell, she's not used to not being at my side, even though she has my nephew to look after now. She's worried. I get it. It's just—I don't know. I miss her, but we still need space."

The toaster oven dinged. "Hold that thought." He brought her the plate, then fixed her a glass of the rosé she seemed to be rationing. She groaned with pleasure as she tossed back half the glass to wash down the first bites she'd taken of her enchilada.

"Oh, god. This is so good."

"You were saying, about your mom?"

"It's nothing. I'm not moving back to Rhode Island. My family can't move here. I'm definitely not moving back to Seattle. Lots of complex, conflicting emotions. You wanna see the heart I operated on yesterday?"

"Uh, sure."

Sloan grabbed her phone and turned to Rafe with a bright smile. It was Avery all the way. "Today we're going to learn about coronary artery bypass grafting." She held out her phone and, sure enough, there was a human heart right in the middle of an open chest cavity. It was pretty fucking gross, but Rafe sat back and let Sloan tell him all about the procedure she'd successfully performed.

Rafe understood about a fifth of what she said. His GED didn't cover advanced medical knowledge. Still, he liked the way Sloan lit up when she enlarged the picture and walked him through the procedure. He might never fully understand the issues she was having with her mother, but Pauletta Copeland could not deny that Sloan had found her calling.

"I can't imagine cutting someone open, let alone fucking with their organs."

"I mean, I didn't fuck with his organs. I fixed it."

"Sorry. Poor choice of words. I would not trust myself to even attempt to fix someone's organs. Can I offer the lady more wine?"

Sloan smiled, "No, I'm good."

"More water then?"

"I will take more water. Thank you." Rafe felt her eyes on him as he took her plate and her wine glass over to the sink, then got her more filtered water. "This isn't a part of your job," she said when he joined her back at the island.

"It's a part of the other job I might want to interview for."

"What job is that?"

"The man in your life," he said with a little cock of his head.

"Woooow."

"What? What's the problem? Why won't you let me be great?"

"Yeah, I'm the only thing holding you back."

"Heating up food for you and hearing about your day is not some kind of hardship."

"I know. I just—you don't have to."

"Maybe I want to."

They were quiet for a moment, just listening to sounds of the Dodgers pull ahead in a 3-2 lead. The whole setup was pretty simple. Two people sitting together. While Rafe was aching to get between her thighs again, he could also admit to himself that he'd been hoping they'd catch a moment like this.

"Avery challenged me to a fist fight this morning."

Sloan pressed her knuckles to her lips before she turned to him. "She's going to get kicked out of Whippoorwill before lunch time. Are they driving you insane? You can tell me."

"The hard part is not laughing. Avery's funny."

"Oh my god. Now you know my pain. We were at Trader Joe's and this rude White lady cut in front of us in the checkout line. Avery told her to get to the back of the bus because we were there first. The cashier and I just stared at each other. We were both dying inside. I had to tell her to be nice 'cause she's gonna end up in jail or worse, but it was hilarious."

"Gracie is just like her. She'll be fine."

"I know, but it's my job to worry."

"If it's okay with you, I'd like to introduce her to WWE. Show her that it's rehearsed. Two of the Bakers' kids were obsessed with a few of the Divas and they had a blast play fighting without actually trying to kill each other."

"That might work. I haven't watched wrestling in ages. Let me check it out first?"

"Yeah. I'll record *SmackDown* for you."

"Thanks. I should head to bed. I'm beat."

"Bed sounds like a good plan."

She stood and closed the small distance between them. Rafe's legs parted, making room for her to get nice and close. "Can I get one of those calm guy hugs?"

"Why not?" The soft weight of her felt amazing against Rafe's body and so did the light squeeze of her arms around his waist. Almost as good as the soft brush of her mouth against his neck and the perfect way their lips finally fit together.

Chapter Seven

Sloan was going crazy. She walked out of the women's restroom at the Century City AMC, Addison's hand held tightly in hers, and she knew she'd fully lost her mind. She spotted Rafe bent over, tying Avery's shoe right near the parking validation machine, and right then and there, she made up her mind. Tonight she was going to have sex with Rafe. Or at the very least, get up the courage to touch his erection.

It was the last Friday before school started and she'd promised the girls that she would take them to the movies. She could have handled them alone, without Rafe's help, but the girls wanted him to come along. As they made their way through the parking garage and up the escalators to catch the six p.m. show of *Piglet's Big Adventure*, she was grateful for the backup. It had been a long, busy week and Sloan was getting used to having Rafe around for the girls' bedtime.

This was something else though. Out in the wild, Rafe really was something to behold and so was the way people reacted to him. Drew was taller than Sloan, but he was still way shorter than Rafe and he didn't have the tattoos. By Rafe's side, Sloan felt like a VIP of the kindergarten set as people practically jumped out of his way to let them by. They got a few stares, but Sloan didn't miss the people who were just straight up checking him out.

Of course he backed Sloan up when Addison started winding up for a soda-related tantrum. He was on the clock. There was stark difference between being home with Rafe and the girls and being out. As they walked out of the theater and he gently slid his hand down Sloan's back, she had the fleeting feeling that she could get used to this, having Rafe with her. Especially after seeing how good he was with the girls and just how comfortable they were becoming with him.

There also seemed to be another shift between Sloan and Rafe. Sometime in the last twenty-fours, after the goodnight kiss they shared, Sloan was starting to feel like it maybe wasn't so crazy for her to be crushing on him and for him to be crushing on her back. Sure, there was a minefield of what the fuck in front of them if anyone found out that she was making out with her nanny, had let him fingerbang her into oblivion and was hoping he would do all that and more the next time they could steal some time alone.

It was more than his insanely good looks or the sexy tattoos crawling up the sides of his neck that made Sloan want to jump him the minute she and Addison came out of the restroom. It was the way he looked at Avery when he held up his massive fist for her to bump. The gesture drove Sloan insane, especially as it had been co-opted over the years, but the way Avery smashed her tiny fist to his and then practically jumped into his arms made Sloan's left and right ventricles work a little harder. It was so damn cliche, but there was something so incredibly sexy about a man who was good with kids, especially your kids.

When he saw her, he shot her a devastating smile, then set Avery back on her feet. "Survived the mad rush to the ladies' room?"

"We did. And now I think it's time to head home and get in bed. How about it, love bugs?"

"I don't want to go to bed," Addison yawned.

"It'll be great. I promise."

They got the girls home and Sloan praised the heavens when both of them were practically falling asleep as she got them in their pajamas.

"For some reason, I'm wide awake," Sloan announced when they were alone, making their way down the stairs. Her tone was as subtle as a dump truck speeding over a huge pothole.

"I hate it when I'm wide awake. Wink, wink," he teased.

"Well, I was going to watch a movie or something, but you don't have to join me."

"I'd considered retiring to my room and mulling over the life choices Piglet made on his big adventure, but I could go for another episode of Horny Millennials by a Pool."

"*Match Made In Paradise*? You liked it, didn't you?"

"After you left the other night, I watched two more episodes."

"Well, now I need to catch up! Let's watch *John Wick 2*. I haven't seen it yet."

"I thought you couldn't do violence."

"I can do, like, stunt martial arts and car explosions. Not tortured, shot in the head at point blank range violence."

"I'm gonna go plug in my phone. You pick a movie with just the right type violence."

"'Kay." Sloan waited a moment until she was alone in the kitchen before letting out the breath she'd been holding. She grabbed some water, then went over to the couch and found the second installment of *John Wick* on her streaming service. Rafe came back a few minutes later. They'd literally been together for the last four hours, but she was still caught off guard by how sexy he was. The beard and tattoos were enough, but there was also a certain swagger in the way he walked. For some silly reason, she saw there was a chance he might not try to sit near her on the mile-wide sectional that took up most of the living room. She was relieved when he made himself comfortable right beside her.

It was time to make her move. "You wanna cuddle?" she asked.

"Fuck yeah, I do."

Sloan moved closer and just being near Rafe again made her feel warm all over. A certain tingling sensation spread all over her body when his arm came around her waist, pulling her right up against him. This is what she'd been wanting all night.

She started the movie and for a while—like forty-five seconds—Sloan was completely enthralled with Keanu and his sweet baby pit bull, until Rafe started slowly moving his fingers up and down, just under her breast. She almost laughed thinking of how right Xeni was. The pussy juice had definitely hit her system, triggering the physiological response that came with pure arousal. Goosebumps, an unmistakable tightness in her throat and the fresh sense of determination followed it. She was getting that dick tonight.

She settled deeper into the couch, resting her head on Rafe's shoulder. Sloan was terrible at dirty talk and definitely not the best at seduction. She decided to let her fingers do the work. Her hand ghosted up his thigh, closer to the crotch of his jeans.

"Is this okay?" she asked quietly.

"Yeah, it's more than okay," he replied. Sloan finally heard what raw arousal did to his already sexy voice. "Here." He shuffled a little, spreading his thighs and pressing further into the couch. Sloan had better access then and she took full advantage, palming him with her whole hand. She'd forgotten how much she liked feeling a man's dick swelling against her fingers. She stroked him over his jeans for a while, listening to the way he was breathing, trying to ignore to how badly her pussy was aching.

When it was clear his cock was straining against the soft denim, she carefully started working on his belt buckle. Inside she felt like she was shaking with need, but her hand was steady as she reached inside the slit in his boxers and took his girth in her hand. He spread his thighs a bit more to make it easier for her to pull his cock out.

She looked up at him as she started stroking his thick erection. His eyes were closed, his red lashes barely touching his skin. When his tongue eased out and wet his bottom lip, Sloan leaned up and kissed him. It must have caught him off guard because he jumped a little, his eyes snapping open.

"Sorry." Sloan sheepishly pulled away, though her hand kept moving up and down.

"Don't apologize. Come here." He pulled her closer and then kissed her properly. Sloan melted against him, pressing her thighs together, trying to ease the throbbing ache in her clit. Unfortunately, it just spurred her own frustrating arousal. She broke their kiss and slid down on the couch. She couldn't take every inch of him, but Sloan gave it her best try, swirling her tongue over the tip before taking the swollen crown between her lips. She'd always loved sucking dick and it been so long since she'd had the pleasure.

She drooled down his shaft, using her hand to spread her saliva down the inches she couldn't fit in her mouth. Her reward was the guttural moan that vibrated rough Rafe's chest. A whimper of her own got stuck in her throat when his strong fingers flipped up her skirt and spread her legs apart. He just barely grazed her clit when she couldn't take it anymore. Climbing over his lap, she straddled him, pressing her lips to his again. His firm grip went to her ass, pressing her against his heavy erection. She humped him shamelessly, reveling in the feeling of his dick rubbing against her cunt through the fabric of her underwear.

A small orgasm ran through her and she had to break the kiss to catch her breath. With the tenderest touch, Rafe reached up and ran his thumb over her lips.

"You okay?"

"Yeah," Sloan breathed. "I, uh—I have condoms upstairs." Sloan had an IUD. Still, she couldn't guarantee that Rafe carried around protection. She'd figured it wouldn't hurt to grab some on her way home from work.

"Yeah, why don't you go grab those." Sloan hopped off the couch, straightened her dress as she casually took the stairs to her bedroom two at a time, slowing down only to tiptoe by her daughters' door. She pulled the box out of the corner of the top of her bathroom linen closet. Her body trembled at the thought of just how good it would feel to climb back across his lap and take him inside her, but just as she ripped two new condoms off the roll, her mom sense activated. She shoved the box back its hiding spot after she heard the sound of tiny feet shuffling across her bedroom carpet.

"Mommy?" Avery called out.

"Yeah, baby—" Avery was standing in the doorway with tears streaming down her face. The condoms were instantly forgotten. "Oh honey, what's wrong?"

"I had a bad dream."

"Oh, sweetie. I'm sorry." Sloan scooped Avery up and brought her back over to her bed. "What happened in your dream?"

"I don't know," she sobbed a little harder.

"It's okay, baby. You're okay. Let's get you back in bed."

"No!" Avery wailed, clinging to her with all her strength. "I want to stay with you."

"Okay, okay. Come on." With a groan, Sloan hefted Avery up and settled against her headboard. She pulled her throw blanket over them both. When she went to reach for her phone, she realized her purse was still downstairs. Great. Hopefully Rafe would intuit the reason she'd just bailed on their sexcapades.

It took some humming, some gentle rocking back and forth, that good mom magic, but Avery finally fell asleep. Just when she started snoring, Addison appeared in the doorway, rubbing her eyes. She didn't even say anything. She realized the party was in Sloan's room and the only logical thing to do was to climb on the bed and make herself

future father of baby #3. There was nothing wrong with any of those options, but she needed to be clear about what she wanted before she had a serious conversation with Rafe. Xeni, best best friend ever.

They'd talked some more and ended up making plans for a girls night in that Saturday night. Xeni and their friend Meegan both had to spend Labor Day weekend with their families and once school started their schedules would be less flexible. Sloan would start up the grill, they'd get in some quality pool time with Addison and Avery, and after they went to bed, it was wine time. It was Rafe's night off, so if he didn't have plans she'd warn him that no fewer than four vivacious young women would be bopping around the first floor of her home.

With her Saturday plans well in hand, Sloan started to get up. Before she could make it to the bathroom, the instrumental version of "What Would I Do if I Could Feel?" from NBC's version of the *The Wiz* started playing from her nightstand. Dammit.

She picked up her cell and hit accept. "Good morning," she said, trying not to suck her teeth. God, she hated her ex so much.

"Hey," Drew said, all cool and calm. "I got an email from the administrator at Whippoorwill."

"With the school calendar, right? I made sure they had your email."

"Yeah. I arranged a parent-teacher conference for the Friday before Labor Day."

"Oh?"

"I'll come down Thursday and then fly them back with me Friday morning after the meeting. I know you won't mind them having a four-day weekend. It's the holiday."

The girls were already staying with Drew an extra night due to Labor Day. He didn't need another extra day.

"Actually, I do. I want them to finish that full week. I want to get them into a good rhythm."

"Listen, you've already fucked up their rhythm plenty by moving. They're only six. Missing one day of kindergarten isn't going to derail their whole lives. Plus, it'll give my mother some extra time with them." And there it was. The real truth. Drew was going to hand the girls off to his mom. Susan was a nice woman when she got her way, but when Drew had the nerve to fight for visitation he should have just been honest about who was doing what when he had them.

"I'll think about it, but I'd really prefer they didn't miss any school so early in the year."

"Okay. Well, I'm coming down to meet their teacher. And I want to meet this dude, Rafe."

"This dude?" Sloan did roll her eyes then.

"Sorry. Your new childcare contractor."

"Anyway. This all sounds great. Come on down and meet everyone."

"You always sound so annoyed and you know what would make this all easier."

"Easier for you and only you. I'm not moving back."

"I'm just saying. My sister said they still had openings at Hyde Country Day School."

Well, have some more kids with someone else and send them to Hyde Country Fucking Day then, she wanted to say, but she bit her tongue. She hated fighting with Drew. It always started off being about the kids and slowly became about how Sloan was incompetent in his eyes, in every way. She'd learned to finally stick up for herself, but when things got that far, when she was pushed to reminding him that she was almost fifteen years his junior and still a better surgeon than him, that all of her accomplishments seemed moot, especially when she broke down in tears. Just thinking about how far this shitty conversation could go was ruining her lovely sunny morning. She threw back her covers and quickly walked out of her bedroom.

"I'm wary of any private school that has openings a few days before the school year is supposed to start," she said, thinking about how shitty it was going to be to see him next week.

"It's a great school."

"I don't doubt it." She stopped near the bottom of the stairs where she was greeted by the smell of bacon. She could hear the girls giggling and that was enough to turn her mood back around. "Do you want to speak to our children?"

"Yeah, I have a few minutes. Put Avery on."

"Fine. Hold on." Sloan dropped her phone to her side, then stepped into the kitchen. The girls were sitting at the island watching something on the tablet. The waffle iron was still out, but the kitchen was otherwise near spotless. Rafe and those blasted sweatpants were surveying the contents of the plasticware drawer. He was also wearing a muscle tee that showed off his glorious tattooed arms. He looked up at the sound of her voice.

"Love bugs, your daddy is on the phone for you." Sloan strategically handed Avery the phone, then walked around the far side of the island just to stop herself from walking straight to Rafe and asking him for a good morning kiss. Still, she felt his eyes on her as she grabbed herself a glass of water.

"You want waffles, Dr. Copeland? I can make you waffles. Cinnamon and nutmeg. It's Monica's recipe."

"I'd love some waffles." She chugged half the glass, then turned away from the fridge, bracing herself for who knows what.

"Morning," he said when she finally made real eye contact with him. She knew there was no medical chance for her to literally combust, but looking at him made her feel like anything was possible.

Chapter Eight

After Avery casually tried to rejoin their post-bedtime, adults only, poolside party twice, Sloan had had enough. She couldn't bring herself to spank her girls, even though her own father had a special belt reserved for such occasions. Sloan instead found that a certain tone of voice deep inside her that conveyed she meant business was pretty effective when it was coupled with actual follow through. This time, the threat of no tablet time for three days was enough to get Avery to stay in her bed.

Sloan understood. They loved Xeni and the minute she showed up with her friends, Meegan, Sarah and Shae, all of whom were great with kids, they felt like they had a bunch of new friends to play with, which was all fun and games until it was time for bed. Sloan wanted to be patient, but she'd also been on edge for hours, ever since she'd gotten off the phone with Drew and she needed to unwind.

Okay, so Drew wasn't the only reason she was on edge. Sloan's work required intense focus. Her patients' lives literally depended on it. It was easy to put Rafe out of her mind for a good portion of the day, but a few hours of carefully avoiding him while craving his touch to a ridiculous degree was making her a little stir crazy. She almost let out a sigh of relief when he went to shower and came back wearing jeans that made her think about his dick a little less.

Rafe had offered to stick around for the bedtime struggle so Sloan could get back to her guests sooner, but Sloan wanted to honor his time off. When she insisted that he flee the scene if he knew what was good for him, he made a call and an hour later, Monica swung by to pick him up. Sloan felt a twinge of something weird when she thought about him spending the rest of the weekend with his family. Whatever the twinge was hiding under its surface, Sloan decided to bury it nice and deep, and keep going on with her weekend.

She made a pit stop at the fridge to grab two more bottles of wine, then made her way back to the party. As she walked through the house, a fresh wave of anxiety hit her. She was new to this friend group and she really wanted to get to know them all better. Meegan and Shae had met though Shae's cousin and her husband. Sarah and Meegan both worked at Whippoorwill with Xeni. Sloan was secretly grateful she'd met Xeni one fateful afternoon in a long Trader Joe's line months before the girls had been accepted to Whippoorwill. There was no way they'd be spending time with a parent of incoming students otherwise.

Shae was an outlier too, but Sloan was sure that the fact that she owned Sweet Creams, one of the best bakeries in L.A., was the glue that kept their crew together. Gourmet cupcakes made everything better. They had been very welcoming to Sloan since Xeni introduced them all, but Sloan was also the only one with kids so she missed out on a lot of their lady hangs. She'd say navigating all of this took her back to high school, but she had no friends then because no teenager wants to hang out with an eight-year-old with a crazy high IQ. Sloan's social development had been so screwed up that even at almost thirty she was never sure if she was doing it right.

She strapped on a smile as she stepped out of the door, then stopped dead in her tracks when she took in the scene on the other side of the pool. Meegan and Shae had been in the deep end when she'd carted Avery back upstairs. Now the four of them were sitting on the cushioned cabana benches, gathered around Meegan. She was clearly crying. Sloan rushed around to the other side of the pool.

"Is everything okay?"

"I accidentally poked a nerve," Shae said, cringing.

"No, she didn't." Meegan wiped her face with a sniffle. "She just asked me about my kinda ex, Shep. Ugh, he wasn't even my ex. I don't know what the fuck he was. He was something though. I— I'll just tell you."

"We don't have to talk about it if it's making you upset," Sloan said.

"No, it's okay. I'm into, like, real kinky shit."

"Real kinky," Xeni mouthed, driving the point home with the face she made. Meegan was being serious.

"I had a thing with this guy, long distance, but he was really good to me. I fucked up and checked his Instagram and he'd posted pics from his honeymoon." Sloan was still a little confused. Meegan had a huge personality, but Sloan didn't take her for the type to sleep with a guy who was with someone else. She kept her mouth shut and let Meegan finish. "It's so stupid. We stopped seeing each other as soon as they started dating, like right when they got together. But it still hurt."

"I know, hun," Shae said in a soothing voice.

"Literally, my last three play partners have gotten married. And then last week my Mistress told me she's retiring, and she and her husband are moving." Yeah, Sloan definitely didn't know what was going on, but she felt awful. Meegan was sobbing even harder. Xeni pulled her close and rubbed her shoulder.

"It's gonna be okay."

"I just—I feel dumped. I knew this was coming, but I still feel blindsided for some stupid reason. It's fucking hard to find a real Dominant who's not just some psycho who wants to hurt people."

"Seriously, I don't know how you do it," Sarah said, shaking her head. "I'd be too scared. Daniel and Keira kind of explained it to me and what they have seems so safe and happy and cuddly. I wouldn't even know where to start."

"I *am* scared," Meegan cried.

"I didn't mean—"

"I know."

"I wish I knew how to help, but I only know the people you know. This is one area where I don't have an in," Shae said.

"Marcos asked me if I wanted to move in with him and T.K.. I love T.K., but I just don't know how not to feel like a third wheel."

"I will literally never have sex with you, but you can move in with me. I'll pet you and tell you you're pretty. But I will never have sex with you," Xeni offered. Meegan finally laughed and her tears seemed to slow.

"But that's the only thing I've ever wanted."

"I know this won't fix anything overnight, but it will be okay," Sarah said. "You'll meet someone."

"I'm sorry, Meegan," Sloan said, feeling a little useless. "Can I offer you more some wine or a cupcake I didn't bake?"

"I'll take both, please."

"Here you go." Sloan topped off her glass of Chardonnay and held out the platter of Shae's cupcakes. She grabbed one without looking and went right for the frosting.

"Look at it this way," Shae said. "You know how much of a mess I was when I met Aidan. I was just desperate not to be alone. I'm lucky he turned out to be awesome. Knowing what you actually want helps you cut down on the bullshit."

"Hear, hear!" Xeni said, with two loud snaps of her fingers. "Be single with me for a while. We absolutely won't have sex and then one day the perfect men with padded bank accounts will magically appear. We'll both quit our jobs and become ladies of leisure."

"Who's the perfect man for you?" Shae asked Xeni.

"A street magician with a long running cable show. Just imagine how much fun you could have with sleight of hand in the bedroom."

"I feel like knowing what I want is almost a curse," Meegan said. "Because what I want is so specific and now that I've figured out that I just want to be with one guy, I feel like there's no way I can find everything I want in one guy. I'm doomed, I say!"

"You're not doomed," Xeni chuckled. "As my aunt likes to say, you're in between blessings."

"Oh yeah?"

"Meegan, you've spent like the last five years with several super hot guys at your sexual beck and call. Plus, Evelyn who spoiled the shit out of you. Now things are changing and you realized you want something different. Give yourself time to find it."

"You're right. I don't know, I think I screwed myself a little. I thought the sex was all I wanted and now I don't know—you're right. Let's talk about something else."

"Sloan?" Sarah asked and immediately Sloan realized her mind had wandered, following Meegan's frantic train of thought. She was definitely making a face. She shook herself.

"Sorry, what?"

"You look terrified."

"Oh, I—" Sloan cleared her throat and glanced at Xeni.

"You can tell them," she replied with a smile. "This is a safe space. A cone of silence surrounds us."

Sloan rolled her eyes at Xeni's hippie bullshit, but decided it was okay to spill the beans. "I'm not sure exactly what it is, but something's happening with me and Rafe, our nanny."

"I knew it!" Meegan yelled. The news seemed to snap her out of her funk. "I saw the way he looked at you before he took off. He's definitely into you."

"It's not horrible if I start something with him?"

"You know what I think," Xeni replied.

Sarah sat back on the cushions and made a show of crossing her legs. "I'm just glad someone is hitting that. I wanted to risk it all every day he came to pick up Winnie. Hell, he's hot enough that Angelo might have let him join us."

"Yeah, he's—pretty tempting," Sloan admitted, though tempting seemed like a really tame description of the way she was lusting after him. "But I guess, listening to Meegan just now, I'm still not entirely sure what I want. My ex was my only everything. First boyfriend, all that crap, and he was also a huge asshole. Is. He's currently still an asshole. I haven't dated at all since we split up. Meeting someone online or in a bar is different than hooking up with your live-in nanny. I think. I've never met anyone in a bar. I'm just scared it's all gonna go horribly wrong."

"It can go horribly wrong with any relationship," Shae said.

"Sure can!" Meegan said with a pitiful laugh.

"I thought I'd married my best friend," Shae went on. "And then, whoops! He finds out he's infertile and everything goes to shit. I literally never saw that coming. But now I'm with my actual best friend who is actually awesome. I never pictured us being together."

"Really, it's not a problem, like school-wise or whatever," Sarah said. "We had a married father of one of our students who was sleeping with four different nannies. His wife decided to confront *all of them* on campus, in front of a large number of children and parents."

"Oh my god. John Hunter," Xeni laughed. "Where are you now? Are you keeping it in your pants?"

"Yeah, I don't think I could be that sloppy." Sloan cringed at the thought. "We're just taking things slow at the moment."

"You like him," Meegan teased.

"I'm really starting to, yeah"

"I can't believe I missed him," Shae groaned. She'd arrived last, after she closed up her bakery for the day.

"I'm sure Xeni has pictures," Sloan said, only half joking.

"Yeah, whatever. My internet stalking skills are creepy until they benefit *you*," Xeni said as she started going through her phone. "Here." She handed the phone to Shae and Sloan watched, awaiting that odd approval that she absolutely didn't need, but desperately wanted.

"Oh, I have a ginger too! And we're both divorced. We should start a club."

"I mean, I'm not sure if I'm ready for full membership, but we'll see."

Her finger moved across the screen like she was looking at more than one photo. "He's pretty hot, Sloan."

"He's a good guy, too." Sarah said with a shrug. "Winnie loved him and he was one the most helpful volunteers I've ever had in my class."

"So, I should lock that down, huh?"

"Yup."

"What are you looking at?" Sloan asked Shae, a nervous laugh following her question. Shae's finger had been swiping quite a bit.

"GodsGracie03's Instagram account?" Shae handed over the phone and sure enough, there was Gracie's Instagram. There were tons of pictures of her with Rafe, Hope and their parents. They looked so happy, and Rafe— he looked so good at being a big brother. She thought of the pictures he'd sent her throughout the week of the girls and how he wasn't in any of them. That weird twinge resurfaced, making her throat feel a little tight for just a moment before Sloan did her best to push it back down again. She handed Xeni her phone and then poured herself another glass of wine. She'd sleep with Rafe first. Then worry about that twinge.

•

After spending some time with his parents and listening to Hope explain all of her issues with the most recent season of her favorite show, *Galaxis*, Rafe headed out to catch up with his boys. There was no plan. Maybe a short ride down the coast. He knew his cousin Marcus would be up to eat, throw a few back and then call it a night. Nothing too wild, since half of their crew had already done time at some point. He also wanted to be on top of his shit when he rolled back to Sloan's house. He was off the hook for Sunday nights, but the girls were looking forward to their first day of school and he knew all three of them would be a little on edge. If he could help make things run a little smoother, he would and he wouldn't be fighting off a hangover if he stepped up to do it.

Rafe parked his bike in front of his cousin's shop, South Coast Tattoo. The CLOSED sign was flipped, but the neon sign above the door was still on. His buddy Hector's bike was parked out front even though there was no sign of him in the front of the shop. Rafe could see the shop assistant, Kendy, sweeping up the waiting area. He walked to the door and gently tapped on the glass. Kendy froze, her eyes narrowing before a bright smile flashed across her face. She set down the broom and came over to flip the padlock. A blast of AC and the sounds of a tattoo gun mixed with a Zapp and Roger classic hit Rafe as he opened the door.

"Hey!" Kendy said, stepping into his arms. "How's it going?"

"Good. Your boss man here?"

"He's just finishing up. You can go back. He's doing a cover up for Eddie."

"Oh, Eddie's here?" Rafe laughed. Monica's other nephew was the comedian of the family. If he was tagging along tonight, Rafe knew they were in for a good time.

"Yeah, Eddie's here!" he heard his young cousin yell. Marcus responded just as fast.

"Man, stop fucking moving."

Rafe laughed, giving Kendy a light squeeze on the shoulder. "I'll just head back."

"Good idea." Marcus's artists tattooed at stations scattered around the main shop floor, but he had a private studio in the rear. He owned the place, so of course the biggest space was his, and he was known for his large-scale black and grey pieces. The larger room gave his clients space to spread out and a better sense of privacy when they had to strip off half of their clothes. Rafe came around the corner and, sure enough, there was Marcus tattooing the right side of Eddie's chest.

"Well, if it isn't Rafael Whitcomb," Eddie said, doing his best impression of a White guy with a stick up his ass. "You son of a gun. How the hell are you?"

"Shut the fuck up, Eddie," Rafe laughed. Almost twenty years of rolling together and Eddie was exactly the same. Sometimes the guy didn't know when to quit, but Rafe wouldn't have it any other way.

When he and his dad crossed into L.A. county with their truck loaded down with all their shit, both personal possessions and a hell of a lot of emotional baggage, they moved into a mostly brown neighborhood. Rafe knew there was a good chance he was going to spend the rest of his teen years getting his ass kicked or getting into trouble, and he'd only been half wrong. Meeting his next-door neighbor Hector had been a blessing and a curse. Hector took Rafe under his wing. Taught him how to break into and hotwire your standard Honda Civic. It was all fun and games until they got busted and sent to Camp Kilgore.

When they got out and Rafe's dad showed up with Monica, Rafe knew his life of crime was over, whether he felt like he still had something to prove or not. Three thousand miles from the streets he knew, Joe leaned on Monica for help. With Hector's mom's blessing, Monica's older nephews sat Rafe and Hector down, and issued an ultimatum. They could all stay friends if they listened to Marcus. Marcus and his friends were cool as fuck, but they all had real plans focusing on trades that would give them the lives they wanted. For Marcus, it was taking over ownership of this shop. Marcus gave it to Rafe straight. He could keep being a stupid little motherfucker and then find himself on the other side eighteen, being charged as an adult for boosting cars or dead for boosting the wrong car. Or, he could surround himself with people who weren't fuck ups and try to do better with his life.

Rafe was still all fucked up with teen rage that he didn't understand how to unpack, but he agreed to stop spending his free time running the streets. When he wasn't watching Hope and Grace, Monica let him hang out with Marcus, his little brother Eddie and their buddies, Nick and Andres, brothers who were training to take over their father's custom auto shop. Neither Rafe nor Hector could draw for shit, so following in Marcus's footsteps were out of the question, but they loved learning everything they could about cars from Andres. As Rafe got deeper and deeper into child care, Hector earned an apprenticeship at South Bay Street Customs and now he was the general manager, helping the brothers expand to a second location in Las Vegas.

"Hector's gonna fight you," Eddie said.

"Oh yeah," Marcus added. "He's gonna fuck you up."

"Why?"

"You got a new nanny gig?"

"Yeah." Rafe looked between them confused, like they'd hadn't been paying attention for the last seventeen years. "It's what I do."

"I saw Monica and she said you were leaving the Mary Poppins life behind."

"I was thinking about it, but—"

"Oh my god, Hector! Stop!" Kendy's screech melted into a giggle just as Rafe heard the bathroom door slam open. Rafe stuck his head out of the door and sure enough, his buddy was strolling across the shop, winking at Kendy. He turned to Rafe and immediately dropped his smile.

"You bitch ass bitch."

"What? What the fuck is wrong with you? Why are you so bent out of shape?" Rafe said. Hector's hostile greeting didn't stop Rafe's old friend from walking across the room and giving Rafe a one-armed clap on the back.

"Carlo got sent up again." Their friend Carlo had not been a part of Monica's ultimatum.

"Jesus Christ. He wants all three strikes. Dumbass. Three months in juvie fucking cured my ass."

"Nick said the same thing."

"Where is Nick? I thought he was coming."

"He'll be here in a minute. He had to drop Junior off at Val's."

"What's going on there?" Rafe asked. His friend and his ex deserved their own reality show.

"Same shit. They hate each other and can't stop fucking each other. I'm waiting for another Junior to pop up any day now."

"Why don't they just get back together?"

"I don't fucking know."

"So, what do I have to do with Carlo?"

"We got a spot at the shop now. I saw your dad and he said you were done nannying and then my mom saw Monica yesterday and she said you'd just signed on with some doctor and her kids. We'd have to get you properly certified, but I could have gotten you in at the shop."

Disappointment hit Rafe hard in the chest. "Fuuckkk."

"Yeah, man. Fuck is right. The two of us, back together on the right side of the law." There was humor in Hector's tone, but he was dead serious. Working together on cars would be amazing and Rafe would have loved to work for Nick and Andres, but he was definitely spoken for now—professionally.

"It was a last-minute gig. Her nanny bailed in the middle of the day and she needed someone to watch her twins."

"What's the mom's deal?"

"Uh—" Rafe started, but the split second he hesitated was enough to completely fuck him. Marcus leaned back and shot him a look.

"Ahhh, shit. She's fine as hell isn't she?"

"She is very beautiful."

"AHHH, SHIT!" Eddie whooped. Next thing Rafe knew, Hector was slapping him on the shoulder and doing a stupid dance in the doorway.

"Moms said she was a single Black doctor, but she ain't say she was fine," Marcus laughed.

"I hope your Aunt Justine wouldn't say that."

"Damn man. A fine doctor," Eddie said.

Rafe nodded in defeat. "She's a heart surgeon."

"Oh yeah, she's not with fucking you. A woman like that? Shit. She needs a business jerk. Serena Williams style. Some internet billionaire to keep up with her," Marcus said before he leaned back over Eddie's chest and continued his work. Rafe didn't argue. Mostly because admitting what had already happened between them would cause him more problems than he wanted. Eddie would blab to his aunt, who would schedule a conference call with Monica so her follow-up questions could be answered properly.

He also didn't want to think about how what Marcus had just said rang so true. Rafe wasn't insecure about his line of work, but there was a difference between late-night sexting and escorting Sloan to some professional medical gala. He shook off the thought that he might not be good enough for her. Her ex was a surgeon and he knew how that turned out. All Rafe had to do was show up for Sloan and hopefully the rest would take care of itself.

Chapter Nine

When Rafe finally called it a night, he considered going back to Sloan's, but he knew his dad expected to get some garage-centric male bonding in on Sunday morning. He owed it to Joe not to bail. He climbed into his guest bedroom bed and tried to fall asleep, but thoughts of Sloan had him staring at the ceiling.

Usually after a certain period of time, the families he worked for took up space in his heart. It was natural. He spent a lot of time with people and since his literal job was to take care of them, he started to care about things beyond their schedules and general health. He cared about their interests, their feelings and after a while, he found that you cared about them.

It had taken a while with the Craigs. He was young and raw, and still getting the hang of the whole live-in thing. He did his job well, but he kept an emotional distance. He didn't expect that working with a family that wasn't his would bring up strange and unexpected issues around losing his mom. Issues he finally opened up to his dad about. With the Bakers, it only took a couple of months. They were warmer and treated Rafe more like one of their own, which was another reason why turning down their offer to join them in Australia had been tough.

With Sloan and her girls, it had taken a whole seven days. Avery and Addison had taken to him so quickly and they were such good kids, it was impossible not to like them. He'd felt a shift at some point during the week, but he knew his feelings for Sloan had painted the whole situation in a different light. His boys had joked about how he was gonna be left a whole chump when she finally met her second husband, but as the night went on he started to notice a familiar feeling settle in his chest. He was grateful for the night off. But while he needed a break from the energy-sapping experience of having two six-year-olds running circles around him, he actually missed Avery and Addison. In the quiet darkness of his guest room, he missed Sloan too.

There was a physical weight that came with adding new people to his life. If they sucked, it felt like being crushed with a brick, but if they were right, he carried the thought of that person around like something warm and perfectly balanced. And when it was gone, he missed it. Yeah it had only been a week, but Sloan and her kids had carved a nice little spot in his heart. Only time would tell just how much space they took up.

He knew there was almost a hundred percent chance she would be asleep, but he reached for his phone anyway.

Hey girl. U up?
Wyd?

If feeling stupid, yet oddly satisfied at the same time were possible, that was how he felt when DELIVERED appeared under his message. He switched over to his sports app and checked the scores from the day, before he switched over to his Instagram to post the one picture he'd taken while he was out with the boys.

I'm up and full of regret.

Why? What happened?

I got a little drunk
but then I started sobering up
and I was tired, but I missed my
optimum sleep window and now I'm
wide awake. Life is so hard.
Did you have a good night?

Rafe wanted to let her know that they did, but he wished she'd been with him. The image of her on the back of his bike, her arms tight around his waist, flashed in his mind. Blood rushed to his cock. He reached into his sweats and adjusted his crotch before he typed out a better response.

I hung out with my pops and Monica
and then I met up with my buddies.

He sent her the picture he'd taken in the In-N-Out parking lot. Marcus had insisted that be their first stop after he closed up the shop.

Oh wow. That looks like a lot of trouble.

We were on our best behavior. I swear.

*We took pictures too. Here's one
where I don't look completely faded.*

A picture of Sloan and her friends popped up on his screen. Rafe had gotten the gig through Winnie's old teacher, but it was weird to see Miss Kato smiling poolside with Sloan. She looked like she'd had a great time. She also looked fucking amazing in the high-waisted bikini she was wearing.

*Oh I should probably ask you this in person
But I'm dying to know.
Are you seeing anyone?*

No. What makes you ask that?

Sloan replied with a shrug emoji.

*I don't know the rules when it comes
To you young people and dating.
You could have seventeen girlfriends.
Monogamy? Rules? What even!*

Rafe couldn't help but laugh. Sloan rambled even over text when she was nervous.

I'm not seeing anyone else.

My last relationship ended about 8 months ago.

Oh. What happened?

Rafe started to give her the abridged version of what had happened between him and Maya, but another message popped up before he could finish typing.

Sorry you don't have to tell me.

I will. It's fine.
She wanted me to quit my job.

Ah, I see. I'm not seeing anyone else
Either.
And I don't want to.
see anyone, but you.
I wasn't supposed to tell you that yet.

Rafe stared at his phone for a few long minutes. He wasn't so sure Sloan had done that much sobering up.

When were you supposed to tell me?

After we had sex. If the sex was good.

Now Rafe had questions.

???

See?!? Us young people and all our dating rules?
It's a mess!

Can I tell you something kinda silly?
That I probably shouldn't tell you.
I'm terrible at secrets tonight.

Please. Tell me.

I miss you.
I like having you here and I miss you.
Even if we wouldn't be in the same
room right now.

Okay, Rafe was positive she was still drunk, but he didn't hate that whatever truth serum she'd chugged was working.

I miss you too.
I wanted to come back tonight.

I know it's your night off, but I would have enjoyed that.
Your arms are warm.

Are you getting tired?

I am. I should sleep.
Goodnight, Rafe.
This was a good talk.

A really good talk.
Goodnight, Sloan.

Putting his phone back on the bedside table, Rafe let out a deep breath. Clearly, the next time he saw her he had to give Sloan the best dick of her life and then somehow explain why they made sense together. If he could make sense of it himself.

•

Sleep coughed up no answers. He still had feelings for Sloan and he still had no idea how to approach the situation. He wanted more than a roommates-with-benefits situation, but also didn't want to rush something that might not be there. All he could do was talk to Sloan and hope like hell they were on the same page. When he went downstairs to fix himself some food, he found Hope in the middle of the living room floor surrounded by a million LEGO pieces.

"Whatcha got going on here?" he asked.

"It's new. Dad found it for me. It's the Millennium Falcon with Rey and Chewie figurines."

"Oh, that's cool."

"We got the royal ship too, from Black Panther. But that one has less pieces so I'll do it as a cool down."

Rafe picked up both boxes and looked at the completed designs, and instantly thought about Addison and her puzzles. His mind flashed back to Hope and her first day of kindergarten. She'd been an oddly serious toddler, with an intense imagination. He'd been worried the other kids would think she was strange, but Monica knew she was tough and that she'd find her way. Sure enough, her love of fantasy became legend on the playgrounds and she became popular with the parents who wanted their daughters around kids with such focus.

"I thought you were sleeping over at Brittany's." Her fanfic buddy from math class was usually attached to Hope's hip.

"I did. They dropped me off an hour ago. Church."

"Oh yeah. That." Weddings and funerals were only times the Whitcomb crew attended.

"It's fine. I'm almost certain that in the cross-section of where science and religion meet, the essence that makes up our souls is safe."

"I like that outlook. I'm gonna grab some food. You eat?"

"Yup." She was already focused back on the pieces in her lap. That was his cue to leave her to her own devices. In the kitchen, his parents were still at the table, enjoying their coffee.

"I made a bacon quiche. It's warming in the oven."

"Oh, I gotta make a quiche this week," he said to himself as he grabbed a mitt and pulled out the half full pie pan. He needed to pick Monica's brain for new recipes before he left for the week.

"I saw Donna Demont last night at bingo. She said Kelly got her discharge." A sharp pain shot through Rafe's neck at the mention of her name. Kelly Demont has been his girlfriend on and off for a few years when he was a walking ball of pissed off testosterone, ages seventeen to twenty. She reminded him of girls from home. Tough, too mouthy for their own good, perfect for the Army. But their last run-in had been fucked up, for a lack of a better word.

All five and a half feet of her had challenged him to a fight and when he refused to punch her in the face, she offered to fuck the man back into him. He'd tried to talk to her about what the hell was going on, but she wasn't hearing it. She wrote him later, during her next deployment, and apologized, but they both knew that relationship would never be the same. Kelly was a good girl deep down, but he wasn't going there. Rafe sat with his food and tried to play it cool.

"Oh yeah? How is she doing?"

"Donna said she's good. She asked about you." Monica liked Kelly. A lot. She liked her for Rafe. "She's thinking about flying helicopters privately. Donna said she's in therapy too." That actually made Rafe relax a little.

"That's a good move for her. She did love being in the air. And the therapy."

"You should call her. Or text her. Send her a tweet or a snap."

Rafe snorted and almost choked. "I don't know."

"Well, if you're not interested in starting things up with Kelly again, I saw Donna Smith last night too. She said Jennifer just broke up with that electrician she was seeing."

"Baby, he can find his own dates," his dad chimed in.

"I know. I just like to hand pick his dates for him. It's my right as a mother. They move out, but I reserve the right to meddle in their love lives forever—until I get the right amount of grandchildren. And then I meddle in *their* lives."

"I—" He didn't need to lie to his parents, but he didn't need to tell them the whole truth either.

"At the moment, my interest lie elsewhere, but my best to Kelly and Jennifer, and their moms."

"There's something going on between you and the doctor," his dad suddenly said, like he'd just found the last clue between him and solving the crime of the century.

"There is... a mutual interest."

Monica shrugged and let out a sigh. "Well. She's a wonderful girl. He could do a whole lot worse. Extremely bright, of course, and she's got a kind heart. I picked that up right away. Plus, her kids are well behaved, so she's got that in check."

His dad put down his tablet and adjusted his reading glasses. "You want my two cents?"

"You know I do. They're worth their weight in gold."

"I am wise. Figure it out now. Let her know what you want, what'cher thinking. The longer you wait, the more complicated and involved it'll get and then she'll give birth to two more kids and you won't know how to tell her you were only asking for directions to the break room."

The air in the room stopped moving as Monica leaned forward so her whole upper body was practically over the table. She tilted her head to the side and her mouth hung open. She looked back and forth between Rafe and Joe. The standoff lasted for what felt like a few weeks. Joe even picked up his coffee and took a long swig. Rafe knew better than to laugh. This was their game and he didn't want to egg either side on. He edged back a little and kept his mouth shut. Finally his dad's lips tipped up in a smirk.

"Fine. I had it pretty damn bad from the moment I saw her and I had to beg her to go out with me."

"I mean! There is no need to lie, Joe!" Monica said at the top of her lungs before she sat down hard in her chair. She sucked her teeth before she turned her to attention to Rafe. "I agree with your no-good daddy. Be good to her, but be up front. If you think you want something more or something serious, tell her. There's no point in playing coy. Not in this economy. Not with this administration. Don't jerk her around, Rafael."

"I won't."

"I mean it."

"I won't!"

"I know she's got the nice house and the nice job and the cars, but the last thing any Black woman needs is a White man making her life more difficult. If you can't be what she needs and what she wants, you leave her the hell alone."

"You have my word."

"*I* don't need your word. She does. Your daddy may be a damn liar, but he takes great care of me. I couldn't ask for a better man. Even if he's full of shit."

Joe stood, making a dramatic show of setting down his tablet, and walked over to Monica. She pretended to fight him off as he planted kisses all over her forehead and cheeks for a few seconds before she caved and kissed him on his lips. Before his mom passed away, Rafe thought his parents had a good relationship, but looking back, his dad and his mom were more like two people dedicated to keeping a roof over Rafe's head.

They never fought, but they were never like this. His dad had real affection for Monica, even when they were giving each other shit. They made a damn good pair and Rafe realized then, no matter how long he stayed working for Sloan, he still had to move on with his life and he didn't want to go through that life alone.

•

Rafe stopped at Target to grab a little something for the girls' first day of school, and more condoms, then headed back to the house. He expected all three of them to be on the floor in an exhausted heap after wash day brought them to their knees. Instead, he was drawn upstairs by the unmistakable sounds of laughter and Beyoncé.

"Hey!" Sloan said when he stepped into the hallway. She was sitting on the floor outside the girls' room, her phone in hand.

"You survived," he said.

"Xeni found a braiding salon on Wilshire that takes walk-ins. Got their hair washed and braided for a wonderful price. Then we went out to dinner. There's a chicken quesadilla in the fridge for you."

"Thanks. Uh, what's all this then?"

"Couldn't decide exactly what to wear on our first day, so the only logical solution was a fashion show."

"Makes sense." He peered around the doorway and sure enough, they'd set up all of their toys and stuffed animals to mimic the audience at a high-end runway show.

"Are you ready?" Avery yelled over the music.

"Oh, we're ready."

Avery jumped out from behind her door, wearing a tutu over leggings and a bathing suit, with three t-shirts around her neck. Her hair was wrapped in a silk scarf covered in unicorns, protecting her fresh style.

"Oh, I love it, darling!" Sloan laughed. "You're giving me fashion, fashion, fashion." Avery walked to the end of the carpet runway, struck a dramatic pose, then turned and strutted back. Addison came next, rolling off her bed in a gigantic wide brim hat that must have belonged to Sloan. She was wearing an Elsa Halloween costume and teddy bear slippers.

"Yes, mama! Work! Work! This is too much fashion."

Rafe watched, a huge smile straining his cheeks until they ran out of steam and outfits. Sloan announced it was time for bed. He helped get the girls into their pajamas as they told him all about their day and the nice women, Sherri and Tina, who braided their hair. They piled into the bathroom for some routine dental hygiene when Avery tossed out one hell of an inquiry.

"I have a question."

"Baby girl, I have an answer," Sloan said as she put away the toothpaste. "What would you like to know?"

"Can Rafe be our daddy at school tomorrow?"

"Uh... I don't think so, honey."

"Why?"

"Well...think of us like a team. My role on the team is mommy and Rafe's is nanny."

"It's a very important role," Rafe added in a weak attempt to back Sloan up.

"Well, you're a mommy and a doctor. Why can't Rafe be our nanny and our daddy?"

"Baby, being a daddy is a little more complicated. Plus, you already have a daddy and he'll be here on Friday," Sloan replied.

"Why can't we have two daddies? One that lives with us and one who's far away? Rafe has two mommies," Addison said, making it clear that the two of them had already tried to sort this out.

"Rafe's situation is different, honey."

"That is correct," he added.

"You're not answering my question. You said that there are all types of families. You told us people have two mommies and two daddies all the time. Why can't Rafe be our other daddy?" Avery said.

"Okay." Rafe replied, like he actually had answers.

"Okay?" Sloan looked at him like she couldn't wait to see how he was gonna solve this.

"I'll explain. So, in this case there are two ways for me to become your daddy. One way is adoption."

"That's right," Sloan said. "We've talked about adoption before."

"It's when you have a baby that you didn't grow in your belly, but you love them just the same," Avery explained.

"Exactly."

"The other way is that I marry your mom. But there are a lot of steps before that could happen."

"What are the steps? I want to hear all the steps." Addison asked, her expression all business.

"Yes, please. This should be interesting." Whose side was Sloan on?

"Step one: we meet."

"Check. Go on." Addison was really sick of his shit.

"Step two: we decide we like each other as more than friends. Steps three through forty-seven involve an intricate process with forms and interviews and off-site visits. I have to prove through another eighty-seven step process that I'm the right husband for your mom and, even more importantly, that I'm the right person to be your dad. You think nannying is hard. Try being a dad!" Both girls giggled at the way his eyes popped wide.

"How many steps is that?" he asked Sloan.

"Uh, a hundred and thirty-four."

"See, yeah. That's a lot of steps. I don't know if we can complete all those steps by tomorrow. But I will be there for you as your nanny, a little bit of light security, snack vendor and driver."

"Rafe is a part of our family. You see that, right honey? He doesn't have to be your daddy to be with us."

"I guess."

"Now let's finish brushing those teeth so we can say goodnight! Tomorrow is a new day and it will be a great day!"

Both girls seemed to give up Operation Daddy and focus back on the new school adventures they faced. After Rafe said his goodnights, he left Sloan alone with the girls and went to start some laundry. A while later, she found him in the kitchen heating up a home plate sized quesadilla.

"I think we should talk," she said, before gnawing on the inside of her lip.

"Yeah."

Chapter Ten

Sloan leaned against the counter and let out a deep breath. When she woke up that morning and looked back on the texts they'd shared the night before, she wasn't entirely sure just how much of an ass she'd made of herself. Rafe seemed to be on the same wavelength. They'd only been apart a few hours, but they'd missed each other. That was cool. Made the butterflies in her stomach do a little dance.

She'd felt a little less silly when the girls had asked when Rafe was coming back a few dozen times throughout the day. They'd wanted him to come to the salon with them. It was Addison's idea to order him some dinner to go.

"Rafe eats a lot. Even if he has dinner with his family, he'll be hungry again when he gets back to our house," she'd announced as they looked over their menus. They were clearly growing closer to him. Sloan should have expected they would want to know more about him, think about him as more of a permanent part of their lives, but she definitely wasn't expecting them to ask her anything that would make her almost choke on her tongue.

Rafe, Mr. Calm'n'Cool, on the other hand, leaned against the counter beside her, his muscled arms crossed over his broad chest like he wasn't the least bit shocked. "Do you want to hear my armchair child psychologist's opinion?"

"Yeah. Actually, I do."

"I'm pretty sure this has more to do with them liking me than them wanting us to be together."

"Really?" She felt her eyebrow go up.

"Yeah. I didn't meet Tess, but something tells me that if she was the type of person to walk out on them in the middle of the day, they might not have bonded with her that well."

"Yeah, I guess. Tess was responsible-ish, but she wasn't as warm as you are with them," Sloan admitted. Rafe and Tess definitely had different approaches.

"I think they see us all together and think family unit," he said. "I'm not downplaying it. It's not nothing. They are thinking about the adults in their life, but it's not something to panic about."

"Well, look at you Sherlocking this whole situation."

He shrugged. "When I'm right, I'm right."

"Yeah, I think you may be onto something, but holy crap. I almost had a stroke."

"Avery's middle name should be 'Keeping You on Your Fucking Toes'."

Sloan laughed and dreaded having to talk to Avery about her own personal drama one day. She could already feel herself greying from the stress. "Well, at least we distracted them with the Truth of A Hundred and Thirty-Four steps."

"About that," he said. Sloan picked the wrong moment to look up at Rafe's gorgeous face. The tip of his tongue slowly crept out and wet his full bottom lip.

"Yeah, about that."

"I've been told that I need to make my intentions with you clear," he said.

Sloan's stomach twisted. If Xeni got a hold of his number... "By who?"

"Joe Whitcomb and his wife, Monica."

"You talked to your parents about us?"

"They forced my hand a little. Monica tried to set me up with two different women at breakfast."

"Uh—"

"I'm not seeing anyone else and I don't want to, but you said there was something we had to do before we could even talk about this?"

"Yeah..." Sloan watched as Rafe turned and stepped into her personal space. She took an automatic step back just so she could see his face, and another as he stepped closer. He followed her, edging her further and further back until she was halfway down the hall to his bedroom.

"I can wait until next weekend, but I really don't want to," he said.

"Neither do I."

"I think we got lucky last week, with that forty uninterrupted minutes. Who knows how long we have now."

"You're right. Knowing Avery, she'll be up in the next five minutes asking if she can drive the car to school tomorrow."

"We should really take advantage of every moment we have," Rafe said, eyeing her up and down.

"We really should. Where are you taking me?"

"I'm not taking you anywhere. I'm going to my room for a second. I left some things in there. You're more than welcome to come with me. Help me find them."

"Well, if you need help, then the polite thing for me to do would be to help you."

"I'd appreciate the help, Dr. Copeland."

"Ooh, I like the sound of that," she said as he slowly backed her into his dark room. "When we finally get the house to ourselves, I might have to give you a full physical examination."

Rafe turned on the light and locked the door. The kids were good about knocking on closed doors, but a lock would buy them a few extra seconds for her to hide under his bed or in the bathroom. He moved closer again, backing Sloan up against the bed. They weren't touching, but she could feel the heat coming off his body. Or maybe it was heat of her own.

"When we finally have the house to ourselves," he said, the sex in his voice hitting her right between the legs, "I'm going to lay you out on that kitchen counter and eat your pussy for breakfast."

"I like—" her voice caught in her throat when he bent down and pulled her yoga pants and her underwear down to the middle of her thighs.

"These are some tight-ass pants."

"You don't like them?" She'd heard that some guys thought leggings weren't suitable for everyday wear, but fuck that. They were comfortable and cute. It took her a second to realize he wasn't complaining though.

"They've been driving me fucking nuts." He leaned down again, scooping her up like she weighed nothing.

Before she knew what was happening, he rolled her on her side, facing the window. She heard a light thud, but by the time she realized it was the sound of Rafe's knees hitting the carpeted floor, he'd spread her thighs apart as far they would go while they were still trapped by her elastic waistbands.

He was eating her out from behind. She wasn't sure he could reach her clit with his tongue from this position, but he could definitely reach her dripping wet opening. There was no teasing. He went at her like a man thirsty and starved. His whole mouth was trying to cover her exposed skin.

It had been so long, the sensation of his lips and his mustache and his beard pressed up against her, pushing, trying to burrow deeper, felt foreign, but so, so welcome. Still, it took her a few more moments to relax, get out of her head and just enjoy the way his tongue was now moving inside her cunt. Burying her face on the duvet cover that now smelled like him, she used the soft cotton to drown out her moans.

Rafe's hand smoothed over her ass, gently squeezing, kneading her skin. It was too much. She started squirming, her hips pumping back and forth. Her body was trying to ride his tongue and give her clit the pressure it needed to make her come. She was so close and then Rafe was gone. No lips, no hands, leaving her cold.

"Rafe," she groaned. "What are you—" she looked over her shoulder to catch a glimpse of something she was sure would be burned into her memory for a long time. Rafe with his shirt tucked under his chin. His jeans open, revealing a geometric pattern tattooed down his side and his large, thick cock, swollen nearly purple at the head as he started to roll the condom on.

"Don't move, Doctor. I'll be with you in just a minute," he said with a wink and Sloan almost died. She flopped down on the covers, trying to fight off the frustration coming directly from her aching pussy and the building anticipation from knowing he'd be back inside her at any moment.

"Do you know how good you taste?" he asked as the bed dipped behind her. She could only answer with an incoherent whimper. He wasted no time pushing inside of her. He didn't rush, but he really wasn't playing around. When they had hours to play, he'd tease her, grind into her nice and slow. She was sure of it, but tonight was not that night. She was ready, so wet that the way he stretched her only eased the ache and amped it up in the best possible way.

He pumped into her, deep and hard. It was good, even better when his hand left where it was holding her steady, just above her knee, and traveled up under her shirt. He leaned over her and she did her best to meet him partway, leaning up on her elbow. His lips brushed against hers. She could taste herself, smell her juices that had just coated his facial hair. It spurred her on and she pushed back against him even harder as her hips moved back and forth against the sheets. His fingers, still searching, pushed her bra up and out of the way. She couldn't wait to see what it felt like to have his tongue swirling over her nipples, but for now his fingers gently pinching and caressing were more than enough.

He broke their kiss. The look on his face cleared and he seemed determined to focus on the only thing that mattered. Making her come. Soon, the thick in and out of his cock was more than enough to send her over the edge. She pushed back on him, hard, clenching around his length, riding out an orgasm that didn't want to let her go. She had no idea how long the shudders of lightning shot through her, but at some point she felt him tense up, and soaked up the ridiculously sexy sound of his moans as he jerked inside of her, filling the condom.

It was a little while longer before she could see and hear properly, but that didn't stop her from letting him kiss her again as they both came down.

•

They fixed their clothes and opened the door, but neither of them seemed in a rush to get back to their Sunday night responsibilities. They sat beside each other on the foot of Rafe's bed, kind of shoulder to shoulder, he was so damn tall. He nudged his foot, still sporting its clean white sock, against hers.

"So, what do you think?" he asked.

"Oh no. I think I remember you saying something about declaring your intentions. You go first."

"Alright. Well, I'm into you. A lot. I'd like to be with you, for real. Try out for the role of being your man."

A new rush of heat spread over Sloan's face as she processed what he'd just said. She thought about everything Xeni had said. She tried to think back to how she'd pictured starting a new relationship and realized she hadn't given much thought to starting something new with anyone after Drew. Her focus had been work and the girls, and getting the hell away from Seattle. None of that had changed, but now there was this new person in her life. She just had to decide if she wanted to make real room for him.

"What do we do about the professional aspect of this?" she asked.

"I don't see why we can't leave it how it is for now. Under regular circumstances, we'd have to tell our superiors, but our superiors have to be up for school in nine hours."

"It's that easy, huh?"

"Unless you're not okay with it, which I totally get. Rejection isn't fun, but I can handle it."

"No. I am...I am okay with it," she admitted. Every reason she could think of not to do this just didn't apply. They were two consenting adults who wanted to give it a go. Every complication she could think of had to do with the girls and those would come up with any person she tried to date. She nudged his shoulder. "So you wanna be my boyfriend?"

"Yeah, I do."

"Okay. I know how this might sound, but can we keep this under wraps until I'm ready to tell the girls? If we decide it's not working, I don't want to them to think they are losing more than a nanny—if you decide to move on."

"I think that's a good idea."

"Good. Are you okay with quickies and panicked fucking except for one weekend a month?"

The deep snort Rafe let out jostled the bed. "I think I can manage it."

"Okay, then we're on the same page. Oh and you should still take your weekends. I know this is muddy waters and all, but you still get breaks from us."

"Who said I was giving you my weekends?" he said, deadpan.

"Oh, it's like that?"

"I'm kidding. I will take my weekends. I've reached that age where I finally appreciate my parents and Hope's off to college next year. I want to get as much time with her and Gracie as possible."

"See, I love that you love your family."

"They're pretty alright."

"I'm sorry about earlier, when the girls brought up your mom, and for bringing her up now. Sorry."

"It's okay."

"They mentioned that you told them she'd passed away."

"When I was thirteen," was all he said. Sloan reached over and squeezed his hand, letting him know that he could talk about it as much or as little as he wanted, but he didn't continue. He just squeezed her hand back.

"Listen, I'll be up for at least another hour. You may have fucked me boneless, but my babies have their first day of school tomorrow and I know I'm more nervous than they are. You want to hang out with me while I anxiously recheck their backpacks and rearrange the whole kitchen?"

"Count me in." Rafe stood and gestured for her to lead the way.

•

Sloan leaned down and looked at them both one more time. She knew she was being overdramatic, but she wanted to press this moment into her memory. She couldn't believe her girls were old enough to start school. Rafe had let her ramble like a maniac until she had to force herself to call it at night. She slept terribly and woke up with more than enough time to get the girls ready for their day. They were all business, going through their list of what they needed for the day together. Sloan had to head off Avery's attempt to bring the tablet with them. Eventually, after she took seven hundred pictures on the front steps, it was time for them to go.

"Okay, my love bugs. It is time for school. Are. You. Ready?"

"Yes, ma'am," Addison said with a bright smile. Avery looked at her, her brow drawn in.

"I was born ready, mama."

"Yeah you were."

"I have a little something for you both." Sloan looked at Rafe as he squatted down to their level. He still towered over them by a good foot, but it worked. He opened his palm and revealed two plastic starfish, one pink and one purple.

"I had some time to think and I discovered another animal that makes the cut for all-time fave."

"You can't have more than one favorite." Avery said, cocking her head to the side.

"Says who? You two are both my favorite," Rafe replied as he handed the Avery the pink starfish. Addison snatched the purple one, turning it over in her small fingers.

"We can keep these?" she asked. "We can take them to school?"

"Yep. Think of it as your good luck charm. I feel like you can't go wrong with a starfish in your pocket."

"What do you say, girls?"

"Thank you," they responded in tandem. Sloan swallowed to keep herself from bursting into tears. "Let's go!" The four of them piled into the Tahoe and they were off.

Sloan could only describe the scene at Whippoorwill as adorable chaos. Rafe helped her unload the girls and volunteered to stay with the car while she got them to their classroom. She spotted Mrs. Brown with ease, in the middle of the kindergarten hallway. She was occupied with a screaming little boy who did not want to leave his mother's side. Sloan glanced down at both girls, but they were in their own world. Calm and focused. Sloan wished she could the same for herself. She was so close to losing it. Her saving grace was standing right across the hall. She made eye contact with Xeni and felt like she could breathe again.

"It's the fabulous Copeland girls!" Xeni cheered. The girls made a beeline for her.

"Hi Miss Xeni," Avery said. "Look at my starfish."

"That is so pretty."

"I got one too," Addison said. "They're good luck charms from Rafe."

"Oh, I'm always on board for a good good luck charm. How are you holding up, mom?" she asked with a wink.

"I'm gonna cry. Is that normal?"

Xeni held out her hand and slipped her a small pack of tissues. "Absolutely. You guys should go find your cubbies! I'll see you at recess," she said to the girls. Sloan walked them across the hall and greeted Mrs. Brown. Sloan bent down and hugged and kissed them both.

"Rafe will be here to pick you up and I'll be home in plenty of time to put you to bed."

"Okay," they both said, Avery with a little more confidence. Her heart nearly split in two when Addison reached over and grabbed her sister's hand.

"Your cubbies are right next to each other. Come on, I'll show you," Mrs. Brown said. Sloan stood in the door and watched as their teacher showed them where they would be keeping their things. After Mrs. Brown directed them to a round table where two other kids were already seated, Sloan knew she had to go.

Xeni was busy talking to another set of parents, but she caught Sloan's eye and gave her a little wave before Sloan headed back out to the car. As soon as Rafe pulled into traffic, he reached over with his free hand and intertwined their fingers. Sloan stayed silent as they took the short trip over to the Medical Center campus. She didn't mean to close Rafe out, but she thought if she said anything she'd burst into tears. When they arrived, Rafe put the Tahoe in park and turned to her.

"You sure you don't want me to pick you up?"

"Yeah. You'll have to pack up the girls and bring them with you. It's more energy than it's worth. I can get a Lyft."

"They're gonna be okay."

"I know. I just wasn't prepared to feel—I don't know. This shit is intense," she said with a shaky laugh. "I feel like I abandoned them to the world. What if there's a biter in their class? Biters are the worst."

"There's definitely a biter in the bunch. There always is, but you think Avery is going to take any shit from a biter?"

"No," Sloan laughed.

"They're ready and you got them there."

"I guess I did. The starfish were a nice touch."

"Tiny pieces of plastic don't compare to the rigors of childbirth and six years of rearing, but I'm sure I'll be mentioned in an acceptance speech at some point. And don't worry, I bought like forty of those things. It's okay if they lose them."

"Good call. I have a consult in half an hour and I have some paperwork to follow up with. I should head inside."

"Can I kiss you or will that get the hospital rumor mill started?" Rafe asked as he continued to stroke his fingers over the back of her hand. Sloan leaned over the center console and pressed her lips to his to answer his question. She kept it nice and PG. Still, a certain kind of heat started spreading through her chest. She was a complete wreck inside, but for the first time in a long time she felt like she wasn't alone. When she pulled back, Rafe reached up and brushed his thumb over her cheek.

"I keep my personal life out of the hospital and I've gotten pretty good at keeping people out of my business. If anyone asks, I'll deflect like a champ."

"Oh, well that answers that. Text me if you change your mind about the ride."

"I will."

Sloan hopped out of the car, feeling a little boost from the kiss they had shared, but as soon as she sat down in her office she was struggling to pull it together all over again. She pulled out her phone and brought up her family text chain. It had been a little quiet the last few days. Everyone was busy. She sent a half dozen of the pictures she'd taken.

They're off!

Before anyone could respond, she called her mom.

"Hold on one moment. My daughter's on the phone. Hello, sweetheart."

"Hey, mom." Sloan couldn't keep her voice from trembling. "Where are you?"

"I'm at Shaw's, grabbing some fruit for Winston." The thought of her sixteen-month-old nephew made her tear up even more. "What's going on?"

"I can't talk long, but I just dropped the girls off at school and I wanted to tell you I get it now."

"Oh, you remember how *I* cried your first day of school and you told me to be cool? You had it under control?"

Sloan laughed as tears started running down her face. She'd given birth to double the payback for all the days she'd given her mom a hard time. "I vaguely remember that, but that's not what I meant. I get why you stuck with me until I got all the way through. I wanted to stay with them too."

"What's the phrase the kids say? You've leveled up in motherhood."

"Yeah, it feels sort of like that."

"It's part of the journey, baby girl."

"I know. I should go, but I just wanted to slip you a well-earned I told you so."

Her mother let out a snort of laughter. "Well, I appreciate that."

After they said their goodbyes, Sloan ended the call. When she clicked back out to the home screen, her dad and brother had replied to her texts.

Gordy: They look cute as hell, Sloan

Dad Copeland: I just wanna know when they're gonna get jobs. Old enough for school. You're old enough to work.

Soon dad. Don't worry.

Sloan slipped her phone in her pocket before she wiped her cheeks. She had patients to see.

Chapter Eleven

Monday Night

Rafe grabbed some of the massive, hotel-style towels Sloan stocked in the linen closet and helped Addison and Avery out of the tub, one by one. The girls had been fucking amped when he picked them up from school. The hustle and bustle of Mrs. Brown's kindergarten classroom seemed to work for them just fine, but they were so hyper, he had to match that energy throughout the afternoon just to get them to mellow out. Sloan would have killed Rafe if he let them go in the pool with their freshly done braids. The elaborate low pigtails were slicked down with what she made sound like a gallon of gel. She'd given him a quick tutorial on how to smooth down their parts if needed, but he couldn't smooth down a dunk in a pool.

He'd let them buzz around the driveway on their scooters until they were out of breath and then fed them Italian for dinner. They were both listing a bit to the left by the time their bath rolled around. He knew they'd be out cold as soon as they hit their pillows. Just as they finished brushing their teeth, he heard the door downstairs slam closed.

"Hello?" Sloan called up the stairs.

"Mommy!" Avery spun on her heels and bolted out of the bathroom. Addison hung back, seemingly waiting for him.

"You alright?" he asked, taking her little hand. She adjusted her pink shower cap with the other.

"I'm just exhausted," she said with a dramatic sigh.

"I get it. You've had a busy day. Let's go say hi to your mom." Out in the hallway, Avery was already telling Sloan about their day. "Hi, baby." Sloan kissed Addison on her cheeks. "Oh, you smell so good. Come on. Let's get your pjs on," she added, directing the party into their bedroom.

"Mommy, will you put lotion on my back?" Addison asked.

"Of course I will. I want to hear more about your day."

"I got to help hand out the crayons. And we both got stickers for sharing because we shared with Marlin and Seth. They're our new friends. They sit at our table."

"New friends and stickers. That sounds like a great day."

"Seth is having a birthday party and he invited the whole class. Can we go?"

"Of course you can."

"Can we have a party for the class for our birthday? I asked Rafe, but he said we had to ask you," Avery said.

Rafe saw the horror in Sloan's eyes as she scrambled to come up with a quick answer. He knew the standard, invite one kid you gotta invite them all, but he also knew what

Sloan was picturing. Twenty-some odd kids and their parents filling up her house, testing the safety of her pool deck. He'd be there to help out though, and maybe he could kick Gracie a few bucks to pitch in. "Uh, I guess. Sure. That should be fun."

Rafe hung around through story time, then said his goodnights, leaving Sloan to get a little extra cuddle time in with her girls. He cleaned up the bathroom, threw in a load of laundry and started the dinner dishes when Sloan came into the kitchen. She'd changed into a loose pair of sweatpants and one of those skin-tight tank tops with the thin straps. She'd twisted her braids up in a pile on top of her head. A real casual look, but Rafe wanted to rip her clothes off.

It didn't help his hard-on that her tits looked fucking amazing under the dark pink fabric. It showed off the outline of her hard nipples perfectly. He held back a sigh of relief when she walked right over to him and wrapped her arms around his waist. He'd spent the whole day working real fucking hard *not* to pine after her like a teenager. He'd failed, but there was an attempt. Leaning down, he kissed her on the temple. She smelled like citrus. She nuzzled closer and sighed.

"I've been wanting to do this all day."

"You hungry?" he asked.

"Did you cook?"

"Shit yeah, I did. Spinach lasagna."

"Oh, that sounds so good. It's in the fridge?" she asked, heading in that direction.

"Middle shelf."

"Score." Sloan fixed herself a plate while Rafe cleared out the sink, then they both grabbed a seat at the island.

"How was your day?" Rafe asked as she washed down her first bite with some water.

"It was...hard."

"Do you want to talk about it?"

"We're operating on this girl tomorrow. She's twenty-two. We're doing a valve replacement. It's gonna be fine, but she is terrified. We walk her and her parents through the procedure, answered all of their questions and she just loses it. Not screaming, but so many tears. Like tears just leaking out of her face and it wasn't so much jarring as it was sad. I could see how genuinely scared she was in her eyes. It's—there's this thing there where people fear something worse than death."

"Yeah, that fear of the unknown."

"Yes! People generally aren't excited to be operated on, but I just felt awful because she was so, like, distressed. I guess I just have to make sure I don't fuck up royally."

"You won't."

"I know. I'm that good."

"See."

"No, I work with a dream team. We've got it under control. Also, work kept my mind off thinking about how I can install cameras in Mrs. Brown's classroom. I was freaking out so bad I called my mom after you dropped me off."

"See, that fear of the unknown hits us all. When I went for pickup, Mrs. Brown said they had a great day."

"How was your day?" she asked.

"Good. Hit the market. Hit the gym—" Rafe looked down at Sloan's hand as it moved to his forearm, tracing the the biomech tattoo that covered his skin. His muscles twitched at her touch, but he kept still.

"I kinda like the idea of my boyfriend hitting the gym and then making really good lasagna."

"Is it good?" he asked, nodding toward her plate.

"You know it is. How many tattoos do you have?"

"One," Rafe teased. "It's one giant tattoo. Took sixty straight hours."

"Ha ha. Seriously."

"I've lost count. A lot."

"Are you going to get more?"

"Every time I chaperone a field trip and lose a child, I get a tattoo. A celebration. Like I've done something right."

"Oh my god," Sloan said, giving him a playful shove. He caught her hand, pulled her a little closer and then he kissed her properly. It was quick, but a perfect kiss right on her soft lips. When he pulled away, it was clear from the look on her face that the kiss had hit her the same way. "You're awful."

"I get one when I'm moved to get one. When I'm inspired."

"I'm afraid it would hurt too much."

"Hurts a lot, but that's part of it."

"Do you like pain?" she asked. Her tone sounded a little unsure.

"Not like that."

"Oh, okay. Not that there's anything wrong with that. I could pinch your nipples really hard if I thought you were into it, but I don't think I could bring myself to hurt you, hurt you."

He knew what she meant, but he did consider other interpretations of the sentiment for a second. "That's very sweet of you, Doctor. I appreciate it."

"When I'm done eating, I'm gonna brush my teeth and then you wanna make out with me while we watch Horny Millenials By A Pool?"

"Yeah. Let's do it."

Tuesday Night

Sloan gently closed the door to the mudroom and stepped out of her clogs. She was expecting the usual silence that greeted her when surgeries went long, and dinner and bedtimes had to go on without her. What she heard was the unmistakable voice of Niles Crane. In the living room, Rafe was stretched on the long end of the sectional. She thought he was asleep for a moment, but as she reached for the remote, he turned and looked at her.

"Hey." The afterhours bass in his voice almost took her out. She wedged herself in the small space at the edge of the cushion. Her hand drifted to his tight stomach.

"Did you wait up for me?"

"Yes."

"You didn't have to."

"I wanted to."

"How were the girls today?"

"Good. I think they're really enjoying being around more kids." Sloan felt bad and relieved all at the same time. They'd met a few kids at the park and through their dance class, but Avery was more into running in circles than actually dancing and Addison didn't feel like dancing with an audience. After she let them drop the class, Sloan hadn't been the best at getting playdates together.

"That's good. They're so good at keeping each other entertained that I dropped the ball at trying to throw other kids into the mix sometimes."

"How was your day?"

"Good. The girl I told you about? There were complications, but we got through it. She'll be fine."

"I can't imagine how stressful that must be."

"You'll see. Wait until Addison and Avery get sick at the same time. That will be a test for you, young man."

"I can't wait." Rafe sat up and stretched.

"Where are you going?"

"I was going to bed, but I think that's the wrong answer."

"Complete wrong answer." Sloan leaned forward and kissed him on the mouth. "Will you cuddle me for a little while? I like the way I feel wrapped in your big strong muscles."

"Oh yeah?"

Sloan laughed quietly as he made his pecs dance. "Come here." Sloan climbed on top of him and settled her weight against his as he wrapped his arms around her.

"I missed you today," she whispered as she peered into his blue eyes. "You know how when you click out of an app, but you don't close it and it's running in the background of your phone?"

"Yeah."

"That's kinda how my brain is when I'm operating. That's the app at the forefront, but then all these other apps are running in the background. I feel like I've downloaded your app and it's running in the background all day now."

Rafe just stared at her, saying nothing. Sloan started giggling and the longer he stared, the harder she laughed. She buried her face in his shoulder and laughed uncontrollably.

"Sloan."

She laughed even harder, shaking her head. She'd die from embarrassment before she looked him in the eye.

"Sloan."

"I can't."

"Sloan."

"No, I won't. I refuse," she said, even as she looked up anyway. "Do you understand that I could have said something so much cornier?"

"There was something worse?" he asked with a straight face.

"Oh, so much worse. I won't tell you what exactly, but it does involve the word 'giddy'."

"I see," he said, before his expression softened. He reached up and lightly ran his thumb over her cheek. "I thought about you all day."

"You did?"

"Yeah. You were the only app at the front of my brain phone."

"Yes, bitch. That's just what I wanted to hear." Sloan snuggled closer, taking in the warmth from his body. She didn't really relax until he placed a few kisses on her face. They lay on the couch together, letting the Frasier rerun play until the end of the episode and then Sloan knew it was time to call it a night.

"Let me at least walk you to the stairs," Rafe said, as he turned off the TV.

"You're such a gentleman." They crossed the living room, hand in hand, then Sloan climbed to the third step and turned to drape her arms over his shoulders. She still wasn't eye to eye with him. "Goodnight," she whispered.

He moved to the first step, pulled her closer and then he kissed her. Sloan had given her whole adolescence to studying medicine, but that didn't stop her from dreaming of what it would be like to go on a date with a boy, have him bring her home and kiss her goodnight on her parents' front porch. There had been plenty of times when she'd been bitter as hell about missing out on that. Instead, she'd jumped right to sneaking around with Drew, visiting him at his condo. But this, kissing Rafe on the carpeted stairs, illuminated by nightlights, was so much better.

They exchanged another set of goodnights and another long kiss before she forced herself up the stairs. Sloan checked in on Avery and Addison, then changed and climbed into her bed. She'd missed the girls like crazy when they went to stay with their dad in a few days, but she couldn't wait to finally spend the night in the same bed with Rafe. She couldn't wait to wake up in his arms. In the back of her mind—her brain phone—she couldn't help but wonder how long it would be until they were in the right place to change sleeping arrangements permanently. Instead of dwelling on how badly she wanted that to happen, and how it was way too soon to be thinking in that general direction, she decided it was best to try and get some sleep.

Wednesday Night
A conversation with Xeni via text

I am so fucked.

Why? What happened?

*I got back from work. We put the girls to
bed and then we had a quickie in the pool shed.
Then we came back in, put on MMIP
and shared a pint of ice cream
Then we made out for a bit.*

Oh so you meant literally.

*I can't keep my hands off of him
I don't know what's wrong with me.*

So the sex is good then? Still good?

*The sex is amazing.
And I think it's just getting better
because we feel more and more comfortable
with each other.*

I'm not seeing a problem.

I'm such a dick. I keep talking about him.

What's going on with you?
How's school?
How's the fam?
How are Meegan and the girls?
Any sign of any sexy street magicians?

You're fine. You're actually distracting me.
My favorite aunt is sick.

Oh shit. Babe, I'm sorry.
Which aunt is it? Sick how?

My aunt Sable.
The one who lives in New York. My Witchy Twin.
My fave. She has stomach cancer.

Fuck. I'm so sorry.
Please let me know if I can help.
I'll make some doctor related calls.
I don't know anyone upstate, I don't think
But I know some people in the City.
You know I'll make those calls.

Thank you. It's early so she could be fine
It's just shitty cause cancer is shitty and it's also shitty
cause she's still beefing with pretty much
everyone in my family but me.
Fifty years is a really long time to hold
a grudge, but what do I know.
Please keep talking about Rafe.
I don't want to think about this right now.

You want me to call you?

No it's okay. I'll have a dramatic cry
about it on the beach during the new moon,
But thank you.
Please, keep talking about your man.

Okay.
I'm sprung like a motherfucker.

Xeni replied with a laughing emoji.

He's just so here. Like coming home to him
every night. It's amazing. He's so sweet and he's a good
cook.
And the girls freaking love him.
I'm sure we'll have our first fight and it'll be
a fucking blow out and I'll never want to speak to him
again.

I don't know.

You don't know what?

About you having a blowout with him unless you've got
some insane temper I don't know about.
I've been watching him like a hawk. He stops and says hey to
me during drop off, but not in a skeezy cookie grabbing way.

Like he knows that you and I matter to each other and
that matters to him.
And there's just something about him.
You may be right, boo. I think he's actually just a good guy.

You're fucked.

Shit. What am I gonna do?

Kanye shrug *Fall in love I guess.*

Thursday Night

When Sloan stepped into the mudroom this time, she was greeted by the boys on *SportsCenter* listing off the stories they'd be covering at the top of the hour. She was exhausted. Drew would be arriving in the morning. That was enough to set her twitching. Her day had been filled with trying not to think about his cocky face, two operations and a run in with an asshole of a resident had filled her day.

The minute she realized Rafe was still up waiting for her, heat flooded her whole body. She stepped into the living room. She wanted to greet him, say hey, tell him it was nice to see him, but her voice was trapped in her throat.

He was sitting at the edge of the couch in those damn sweatpants, and nothing but those sweatpants, his feet planted in the carpet, thighs spread wide. She looked him over, checking out the thick muscle that ran up his side and over his shoulder, covered in ink. He looked up from his phone and when his eyes met hers, Sloan knew she was in a world of trouble. The good kind.

A bit of a whimper escaped when he stood and tossed his phone on the couch. Her eyes darted right to the unmistakable bulge pressing against the heather grey fabric of his pants. Sloan slowly started backing into the kitchen. It felt like it took nothing but two steps for him to cross the room. She gasped as his hands went to her ass and lifted her up. Her legs went around his waist, driving his cock right up against her aching cunt. Her arms went around his shoulders, pressing her breasts and their now sensitive tips against his deliciously bare chest. Their lips met, their tongues finding each other in an instant.

Sloan felt herself being carried backward and a tiny thrill rushed through her when her butt hit the far counter. It was risky with the girls upstairs, but she couldn't bring herself to care. She was gonna fuck Rafe right here and right now.

He pulled back, breaking their kiss just enough to get to work on the zipper on her slacks.

"What's come over you?" she teased.

"You want the truth?"

"Yeah."

"I watched porn for a few minutes, like an idiot, and then all I could think of was bending you over in the pool shed again. I've been hard for two hours."

"Oh, we have to do something about that." Sloan reached down and slipped her hand into his pants. He was so hard and hot, but she only got to enjoy it for a whole half a second before he lightly took hold of her wrist, stilling her fingers in their path.

"Sloan. Please," he said, pretending to be annoyed. "I'm about to blow my load. At least let me get inside of you before I embarrass the shit out of myself."

"Sorry," she replied with a little snort. "I'll just let you handle this."

"Thank you." She went to work on wiggling out of her slacks while he pulled a condom out of the pocket of his sweats. He pulled out his cock and slid the protection on. She decided to help him out by tugging the crotch of her underwear to the side. Arching her hips, she took him all the way in a single thrust.

"Fuck, thank god," he groaned.

"Better?"

He answered by pressing his lips to hers.

Chapter Twelve

The doorbell rang and Sloan felt like she was gonna throw up. Two hours max. She had to be in Drew's company for no more than two hours and then she could go a few more months without seeing him face to face.

"Avery, that's your daddy. Will you go let him in please?"

"Okay," she said with medium enthusiasm.

"Thank you." Both girls had asked more than once if it was completely necessary to spend the holiday weekend with their dad. The only thing that convinced them that it would be worth the flight was the reassurance that Drew's mother was most certainly going to bake them cookies and take them on at least one adventure around Seattle.

"I'm done!" Addison announced, handing Rafe her breakfast bowl. A second later, Avery came shimmying back into the kitchen. Drew was right behind her. Sloan wished she didn't have a visceral reaction to her ex-husband, but any time she was near him she felt like a trapped and wounded animal. She'd chew her own leg off to get away from him. He was handsome as hell and dressed his ass off, but god he sucked.

"Hi Daddy," Addison said as she walked over and gave him a hug.

"Hey, A.D.." Addison hated that nickname, which was enough to make her little girl cringe, but then he rubbed the fucking top of her head, against her part? Addison jerked away, smoothing her hair back down and shooting Drew a look that would have earned her a stern talking to from Sloan. In this instance though, Sloan didn't blame her. And of course it didn't matter. Drew was staring daggers at Rafe. "You're the nanny?"

"I am. Rafe Whitcomb." He reached over the island and held out his hand. Drew shook it with a ridiculously hard tug, but Rafe wasn't fazed by it.

"Dr. Drew Ballos."

"Good to meet you."

"You a Boston boy?" Drew said. Sloan had no idea why Drew was talking like that, like he was about to ask Rafe if they could settle all this—whatever this was—with an arm wrestling match. Rafe had not signed up for whatever imaginary pissing contest Drew seemed intent on. Especially in front of the girls. They were both dead silent, watching their dad react to their nanny. Rafe schooled his features, then answered Drew's question.

"Yeah. Grew up right outside, but I've been out here a while."

"Oh, so you're both a long way from home." Drew gestured between Sloan and Rafe. "That's something you have in common."

"Lord Jesus." Sloan was done. "Girls say goodbye to Rafe while I get your backpacks."

"Bye Rafe!" They both ran around the island and swarmed him.

"You got your starfishes?" he asked.

"We keep them in our backpacks so we won't lose them," Addison said.

"Smart. I'll see you on Monday?"

"We'll bring you something from the airport," Sloan heard Avery say. Rafe let out a little laugh.

"Sounds good."

She didn't want to rush them, but they needed to get over to the school and she wanted to get this hellish experience with Drew over with. "Rafe, keys to my car are on the hook."

"Sounds good."

"You're letting him drive your Benz?" Drew asked.

"Yes. I forgot I made an appointment to get it serviced today instead of tomorrow. He's doing me a favor. Why don't *we* get going?" Sloan said. She'd stab Drew one day and she'd enjoy doing it. Especially after he looked back at Rafe and kept fucking talking.

"I heard you ride a motorcycle."

"Yeah. I have one."

"What kind?" Drew asked like he knew a fucking thing about motorcycles. He wasn't even a car guy. He was a boat guy. Boats.

"Ducati Monster. You ride?"

"No fucking way."

"Drew!"

"Oh, sorry." He had the nerve to look guilty for swearing in front of the girls for a moment before he pressed on. "I don't. Road rash is no good for a surgeon's hands."

"Make sense." Rafe was done too. He turned to Sloan, then nodded to the mudroom. "You need help with the bags?" Their little weekend rolling bags were by the mudroom door.

"No. We got it, bro."

Sloan clenched her back teeth. She would not punch Drew in the face in front of her children. "Yes, please. Can you put them in the trunk? Drew can you help Avery with her car seat?"

"Yeah, let's do this." Sloan couldn't look at Rafe before they left 'cause she was afraid she'd run into his arms for a last bit of comfort. Or worse, she'd kiss him goodbye.

"We're going in early?" Addison asked as Sloan strapped her in to her car seat.

"Yes, baby. You're going to hang out with Miss Xeni while your daddy and I meet with Mrs. Brown."

"Okay," she replied with a big smile. They didn't get the levels of sheer fuckery, but her girls were observant as hell. They were on the same team. Team Shut the Hell Up Drew.

Sloan climbed behind the wheel, then queued up the girls' favorite playlist and saved them all from any conversation on the way over to Whippoorwill. Not that Drew would have tried it. He was too busy texting on his phone. When they dropped the girls with Xeni she introduced her to Drew, who suddenly decided to turn on the professional charm. Xeni wasn't fucking buying it. She ignored him and invited the girls to come color. Before Sloan went into Mrs. Brown's classroom, she made sure she

Rafe relaxed a little and leaned against the counter. "You've entered a kid-free zone."

"Okay. First of all, let me apologize for Drew's behavior this morning."

Rafe waved her off with a shake of his head. Her ex-husband was piece of work and a complete dick, but he'd met plenty of dudes like him before. At some point, posturing became a part of their personality. Drew wasn't blameless, not by a long shot, but Rafe refused to waste his weekend thinking about their interaction. He was more worried about Sloan and the girls.

"Are you okay?" he asked. "I know you said you didn't like him, but—"

"Breaking up with someone is hard. Ending a marriage is harder, but people downplay how impossible it is to end a relationship with someone when you have kids with them." She pouted, then dramatically stumbled across the kitchen and into his arms, even though he was covered in flour. "I hate him so much and I can't kill him and make it look like an accident."

"As someone who has been on the wrong side of the law, getting revenge in the form of a happy life is better than murder. Trust me. I don't know how to make anything look like an accident and I'm sure you wouldn't like womens' lock-up. Also, you're hot, but I'm not going back in for you."

Sloan snorted and snuggled closer. "I believe you. And don't worry. Xeni has connects. I'd have her handle it."

"I'm sorry you have to deal with him, but I got your back." Rafe cupped her face and kissed her soft lips.

"That means a lot. Thank you," she said, before she looked him up and down. She frowned, then turned and looked at the center island. He hadn't mastered the art of cleaning as he went.

"I'm about to take care of this."

She turned back to him and smiled. "Were you baking?"

"My extra flaky pie crust needs to chill for at least twelve hours."

"You're baking pie from scratch?"

"Quiche. For breakfast tomorrow."

"Oh my god, I might have to marry you." She stepped back and hopped up on the far counter. Rafe couldn't help but think about how they'd fucked in that exact spot just the night before. He'd also never forget the sound of Sloan's laugh has she cleaned the counters with Clorox when they were done. She cocked her head to the side and bit the inside of her lip before she shot him a seductive smile. "Do you have any other plans this weekend? Besides serving the perfect quiche."

"Do you?"

"Do *you*? My kids are gone. You have two full days and three nights free. You're off the clock, Mr. Whitcomb. I am in no position to tell you what to do with your time."

"That's true. I was thinking about spending some time with the woman I just started seeing."

"What a lucky girl."

Rafe shrugged. "You could look at it that way. I think I'm the lucky one."

"Such a flatterer. Literally all I want to do this weekend is have uninterrupted sex all over the house."

"I'm down with that plan. When we aren't having sex, I was hoping to take you out on a real date and my parents are throwing a block party on Sunday. We could go to that if you're interested."

"Both sound great. I haven't been on a real date in two hundred years and I'd love to hang out with your family."

"Some of my buddies will be there too."

"You're ready to introduce me to your friends?"

"I mean, I met your friends. Only seems fair."

"You're absolutely right. I'm gonna shower and then we can sort out dinner?"

"Sounds like a plan." Rafe watched Sloan as she hopped off the counter. When she disappeared around the corner, he got to work cleaning up the kitchen island. He didn't get very far before Sloan's face peeked around the corner again. "How can I help you, doctor?"

"When you're done here, feel free to come join me. In the shower."

"I'll be right up."

"'Kay."

Rafe hated shower sex, mostly because his six-five frame barely fit in most showers, but Sloan's invite was all he needed to hear for all the blood in his body to start making its way to his crotch. He cleaned the kitchen in record time, then stopped in his bedroom to grab a few condoms before he made his way upstairs. He'd only been in Sloan's bedroom to deliver her purse and some clothes that had gotten mixed in with Addison and Avery's laundry. It felt a whole lot different to be invited.

Just the sound of the rushing water made Rafe's cock swell even more. He stepped into Sloan's massive master bathroom and immediately realized shower sex wouldn't be a problem. She looked small in the huge shower that ran the length of the wall. The ceiling was almost as high as the vaulted ceiling in the bedroom, but even if he'd been dealing with a shitty stand-up shower stall, it wouldn't stop him from joining her under the warm spray.

Rafe hadn't had a chance to see her completely naked in good lighting yet and fuck was he glad they'd finally got some real time alone. The sight of her beautiful brown skin soaking wet, white soapy suds slipping down her body. Her braids were piled high on her head, safe from the water. She'd already wet her face and Rafe caught a glimpse of a few drops running down her chin.

"You coming in?" she asked.

Rafe didn't respond. He just watched the smile spread across her face as he started peeling off his clothes. Once he was undressed, he pulled a condom out of his jeans' pocket and stepped in the shower behind her. She dropped the washcloth she had in her hand on the marble shower seat and set about rinsing off. Rafe was content to watch, stroking himself as her hands moved up and down over her heavy breasts, again and again, until one hand started its journey south.

"Uh uh," Rafe said, sounding like a caveman who wouldn't be denied. He grabbed Sloan's hand and pulled her closer. He spun her and pressed her back and her perfect, round, tight ass against him. He heard her gasp, and it only spurred him on. His hand slid between her legs and fuck the water, but she was wet as hell. Rafe moved his fingers around, spreading her pussy lips even more, lightly pinching her clit.

She made a desperate noise, something between a whine and a moan. They'd been able to sneak in some fun throughout the week, but Rafe had been intentionally holding back. They hadn't had the time or the privacy to do all the things he wanted to do. Like running his mouth over every inch of her body.

Rafe leaned down. Nudging her head to the side, Rafe brushed his lips down the length of her neck. She started squirming, craning her neck even more, swirling her hips against his hand. He brushed his mouth down even farther, giving her shoulder a gentle bite before gliding his tongue over the spot where his teeth had just been.

He kept licking and sucking until he found the perfect sweet spot in the middle of her neck. Sloan arched hard against him, shoving her own fingers between her legs to join him. Rafe gave in, bending his knees a bit to make up for the height difference so he could easily press two fingers inside of Sloan's warm cunt. She spread her thighs, welcoming him into her slick, warm pussy. She rode his fingers until she was calling out his name.

"Fuck, oh my god," she groaned. The sound was enough to force a bit of precum out of Rafe's dick. He had to get inside of her.

He kept his fingers in place and his mouth on her skin until she stopped trembling. She was still breathing hard when he turned her around and scooped her up by the backs of her thighs. Her legs went tight around his waist and her arms clung to his shoulders. If they didn't have real shit to do day in and day out, Rafe could see himself just walking around everywhere with her body hanging off his, their mouths fused together.

"You like picking me up, don't you?" she panted. He looked back at her as her gaze scanned every inch of his face. He was busy taking her in too. Her big brown eyes, her fucking perfect lips. Christ, the dimples. Even her damn nose was cute.

"I think you like it when I pick you up."

"I do," she said and then something passed over her features. Rafe wasn't sure what, but he saw the flicker in her eye and the way her cheek clenched. "Take your time with me," she said. Rafe thought about the day she'd had. The time she'd had to spend with Drew, the years she'd had to spend with him. How he had been her first and only experience with men and relationships.

Rafe didn't know what had been the final thing to push Sloan into leaving Drew, but it had been enough to hurt her. Sure, she wasn't referring to that very moment when her marriage ended, but if she was hinting at something deeper, he was hearing her loud and clear.

"I can make that happen," was his response. A little smile touched her lips before she kissed him. He kissed her right back, giving her thighs a little squeeze as their tongues slid together. Fuck, he loved kissing her. He loved everything about her. He broke their kiss just long enough to move them over to the marble shower seat, and as soon as his ass hit the cold, wet surface, his mouth was back on hers again, savoring every bit of their connection, especially where her pussy was now rubbing up against his dick.

Without pulling away, he reached over on the bench and found the condom. He opened the wrapper and easily sheathed himself. Then he pulled away, cupping Sloan's cheek in his large palm. Her eyes went to his again and this time all he saw was pure lust.

"Do you want to sit on it?"

She just nodded, then reached between them and took of hold of his cock. Rafe let out a groan of his own as she stroked him, her fist moving up and down. Finally she took pity on him. She sat up on her knees, aligning the head of his aching erection with her warm opening. His eyes refused to stay open as she pushed down, taking every single inch he had to offer. Sloan started to move her hips, clenching her pussy around him. Rafe wrapped an arm around her waist and pulled her closer, meeting the motions of her hips with his own.

"You feel so fucking good," he whispered against her ear.

"Oh babe," she whimpered back. "I'm gonna come."

"Come, baby. Come on me." That seemed to be just what she needed. Sloan clung to him, her chin digging into his shoulder as her pussy flexed and released down his length. He held on, pumping into her hard and fast until his balls seized up and that bolt of energy shot up his spine. He filled the condom inside of her as her hips continued to move.

Rafe had no plan to move any time soon, but Sloan suddenly slipped off his lap and moved to her knees on the shower floor. She swiftly, but carefully, slipped the condom off and started to lick him clean. As his dick softened, she kept lightly stroking him, moving her mouth down to his balls. After a minute or so, he lifted her off the floor and kissed her deep. The water was still running, but he couldn't think of a better way to waste some water.

Chapter Thirteen

It should have been physically impossible for Sloan to wake up this aroused, but when she opened her eyes the first thing she noticed—well, the second thing she noticed—was not only how wet she was, but how badly her clit was aching. And this wasn't residual arousal, left over from the last time Rafe had been inside her sometime after midnight, after they'd dried off and lotioned up and pulled together a feast of leftovers that they stuffed themselves with while watching more episodes of *Match Made in Paradise*.

No, this was fresh and urgent. Maybe she'd had a sex dream she didn't remember or maybe some switch in her body had been flipped. It knew quality dick was present and available on-demand, if Rafe was up for it, of course. Maybe she'd be this turned on forever.

After she realized that she was alone in her bed again, she knew she wasn't going to get the instant relief that could come from a morning quickie. It was official. Sloan was turning into a sex addict and the only person who could administer the fix was nowhere to be seen in her bedroom. She'd go find him in a minute, but first she checked her phone. There was a text from Xeni.

Download LetsChat.
We're adding you to our group chat.

Sloan sat up in her bed, gasping out loud. This is what it must have been like to be popular in high school. A hot boyfriend with a motorcycle and cool girls who wanted to be friends with you. She downloaded the app, then searched for Xeni's number.

I'm here! Add me!

Sloan couldn't help but laugh when the group alert popped up. **Xeni has added you to Intersectional Feminists of Benetton.** She accepted the invite, scanning the names at the top of the screen under the perfectly named group. Joanna, Keira, Meegan, Sarah, Shae, Xeni. She'd only had the chance to hang out with Joanna and Shae's cousin Keira a couple of times, but they were very nice.

Xeni: I just added her.

Hiiiiiiiiiii!
Are you jumping me into your lady
violence gang? I feel so special!

Sarah: Hey!

Keira: Hey Sloan! How are you?

I'm great. How are you ladies doing?

"You're up." Sloan looked up as Rafe walked into the room wearing nothing but a pair of boxer briefs. A weird sense of panic made her press her phone to her chest like she was caught doing something wrong.

"Good morning," she said as he climbed on the bed. "I'll be with you in one second."

"Take your time," he replied with a groan. Sloan almost orgasmed watching him stretch out on the sheets beside her.

Keira: Good. Just telling the girls
about my husband's latest work drama.

Shit. Keep telling. I'll brb.

She set her phone on the nightstand and turned back to Rafe. "Hi. Sorry. Just chatting with the girls." She almost melted when his mouth and his mustache tipped up at the corner in a sexy smile.

"Telling them how you drained me of all of my bodily fluids last night?"

"No. I didn't get that far yet, but I will. Imma tell errrbody. How long have you been up?"

"Not too long, but I didn't want to wake you so I put the quiche in the oven."

"What kind of quiche is it?"

"Bacon, spinach and onion. There's fruit salad too," he said before he leaned up and kissed her, reminding Sloan that her pussy was still very much in need of some personal attention.

"Mmm, that sounds delicious."

"I don't think you'll be disappointed."

"So, I have a problem."

"Yeah? What's going on?"

"I'm still wet," Sloan said, shooting her crotch a meaningful look.

"Oh yeah?" Rafe shuffled around a bit so he could get his arm under the covers. Sloan tried to hold still as his warm fingers ghosted over her thigh, but all her effort didn't stop her from breathing in a little harder when his fingers brushed against her slit. "Yeah, you are pretty wet." Rafe pulled his hand away, then rudely licked his fingers.

"How am I supposed to get out of bed like this?"

"I don't know. You might have to stay in bed all day."

"But what about our first date?"

"Yeah, we can't skip that. I think I'm going to have to help you out. Excuse me." Sloan watched Rafe as he threw the covers over his head, then felt as he maneuvered his way between her legs. A sigh escaped from her chest when his tongue slowly parted her lips. Suddenly, he threw the covers off them both and looked up at her. God, it was a sight. His hands gripping her skin, her thighs over his broad, tattooed shoulders, her juices already wetting his beard.

"You were right. It's a mess down here. Cleanup might take a little while."

Sloan reached down and ran her thumb over his bottom lip. "How long will the quiche take?"

"We got about fifteen minutes, give or take. I should get started." Sloan couldn't even respond before Rafe pressed his mouth back to her slit. Jokes about his quiche burning were forgotten as he licked and sucked every inch of her. Sloan settled deeper into the sheets, her head dropping back while her fingers wove their way into the soft hair on the back of his head.

Heaven. This was what heaven felt like, Rafe's tongue tracing over her sensitive folds before pressing into her aching hole. His dick was amazing and nothing compared to it, just like nothing compared to the feeling of his tongue moving inside her. The focused and controlled movement against the inner walls of her cunt pushed her closer to the edge. She felt his thumb slide around the outside of her ass, slick now with her juices and his drool. He didn't push it inside, but just the light pressure had her head digging back into her pillows as she whimpered his name.

A beeping and thrumming noise forced Sloan's eyes up. His phone was dancing and chirping on her dresser. His timer for the quiche.

"Rafe. The oven," she tried to say, but she cried out instead as he sucked her clit into his mouth. Two fingers pressed into her pussy and he worked her, his hand moving in and out in deep, rough motions. The beep and vibrating went on, but Rafe didn't stop, not until she was coming. Lightning exploded behind her eyes as she arched off the bed, pulling his face closer to her. Finally, he released her with a few parting kisses to her inner thighs.

"I'll be right back."

When he climbed off the bed, she didn't miss how hard he was and she didn't miss the wet spot that had turned the dark grey fabric of his boxers black. She knew he'd come back, but Sloan was thirsty now. For actual water as well as more of his body. She jumped out of bed and found her robe hanging in the bathroom, then followed Rafe down to the kitchen. Maybe he'd let her help him out while they waited for their quiche to cool.

•

Sloan leaned against Rafe as they waited for their table at Samba. They'd had a perfect day. After she'd sucked his cock in the middle of the kitchen, they took their sweet time eating breakfast, then decided to take a dip in the pool. They'd spent the rest of the day watching movies on the couch wrapped in fluffy towels. Sloan dozed on and off, cuddled up against Rafe's shoulder, soaking in his warmth.

Eventually they'd unglued themselves from each other, retreating to their own bedrooms to get ready for their night out. After she blow dried her braids, it took Sloan forever to figure out what to wear. When she'd finally settled on a brand new, long sleeved floral romper that she had yet to wear and a pair of tan wedges that she'd barely broken in, she figured Rafe was downstairs watching the clock, wondering what the fuck was taking her so long.

In a shocking twist, it was Sloan that had to wait for Rafe to finish his primping and prepping. She'd had to stop herself from drooling when he came walking down the hall. Rafe always looked nice. Nice jeans, fresh t-shirts. Something about the crisp long sleeved shirt he was wearing and the way the sleeves were pushed up, showing off his tattoos, was too much though. After they'd exchanged seven or eight compliments about how the other looked, they headed out for their date. Rafe drove them in the Tahoe to the Brazilian steakhouse he'd been meaning to try.

Stepping through the front door, Sloan immediately saw why he'd picked the dimly lit restaurant. The whole scene was very romantic. After the hostess showed them to their table and they both looked over the menu, Sloan focused all of her attention on the gorgeous man across from her.

"So, tell me about yourself," Sloan said. "I feel like we've talked a lot about my kids and we've even talked about complicated surgical procedures, but we haven't talked enough about you."

"What do you want to know?"

"Truthfully? Why are you so nice?"

"I don't think I'm so nice. I think I try to be a decent human being."

"I don't know. I think you're pretty sweet."

"I wasn't always like this. I used to be a little dick."

"Really?" Sloan couldn't picture it. Rafe had been nothing but kind and patient with everyone she'd seen him interact with. She couldn't imagine him being an asshole, even as a teenager.

"Yeah, I was a little shithead growing up. Part of why I landed in juvie."

"What changed?"

"My dad."

"Oh yeah?"

Rafe looked down and started toying with the base of the candle at the center of their table. "My parents weren't good together. My dad got my mom pregnant when they were in high school and their parents forced them to get married. They got along, but it was more like a friendship. My dad was just angry in general. But when my mom died, he kinda snapped."

"We don't have to talk about this if you don't want to." She wanted to know more about him, but the conversation had taken a heavy turn and from the way he was avoiding eye contact with her, Sloan could see he wasn't exactly comfortable talking about his parents.

"No, it's good to talk about it," he said, looking up at her. He smiled a little, then let out a deep breath. "It's a good reminder. Anyway. He packed me up one day after the funeral, didn't tell me where we were going. Just loaded up the truck and we started driving. We stopped to sleep and eat and stuff, but he was so focused on getting to the Pacific, I was thinking he was going to just drive the car right into the ocean."

"Rafe," his name slipped out of her mouth and Sloan couldn't help the tone of anguish behind it. She couldn't imagine how scary and confusing that must have been for a young teenager.

"When we got to Santa Monica, it was the middle of the afternoon and the pier was packed. I just wanted to go to sleep in a real bed that wasn't covered in dirty motel sheets, but he made me hang out on the pier while he had whatever moment he needed to have. All he said was that my mom always wanted to come to California.

"We found a place. He found a job and put me in a school where I was one of the only White kids. It wasn't the end of the world, but I really wasn't ready. He didn't tell me we were staying until the night before I was supposed to go to school."

"And you fell in with the wrong crowd?"

"No, I dropped out."

"Oh."

"I met my buddy Hector. He knew this guy who would pay us cash for boosting cars. And that was great until we got arrested."

"I'm sorry, but that is literally the plot of *Step Up*," Sloan teased.

"I know. That movie is based on my life."

Sloan felt herself flinch in shock. "What?"

"I'm kidding."

"Not funny."

"Yeah, it was. Anyway, when I got out, my dad was dating Monica and he was completely different."

"Different how?"

"It was the first time I'd seen him happy in my whole life. First time he'd ever apologized to me. He said he was sorry for uprooting us without talking to me. Sorry for not giving me time to grieve for my mom. He apologized for being a bad father. Hearing him say all that just opened something in me. I told him all this shit I'd never told anyone about being scared to live.

"I didn't know what I was doing with my life. I didn't know who I was enough to even try and be any version of myself, forget a good version of myself. I didn't want to end up dead or in prison for good though. After that, Monica introduced me to her brothers and her nephews who taught me how to work on cars and motorcycles, anything with an engine really. That kept me and Hector out of trouble."

"Are you two still friends?"

"Yeah, you'll meet him tomorrow."

"Good."

"After my dad made it clear that I could really talk to him about anything, I stopped bottling shit up. And being around my new step-uncles helped too. They're gearheads and all that, but as the kids say, they don't engage with toxic masculinity."

"That's great. It sounds like you were surrounded by good people who really care about you."

"That's exactly it. But yeah, I don't see myself as nice. I'm just not jacked up on suppressed rage."

"Hmm. I still think you're nice," Sloan said, winking at him.

"Well, you're easy to talk to. I've had women tell me I'm too quiet and I don't open up enough."

"I don't think you're quiet. You just told me something personal and private."

"Like I said, you're easy to talk to."

"So, how'd you end up nannying?"

"After Hope was born, I was old enough to help out, so I did. Monica said that I was so good with her, you know as an infant, and she asked me to watch her when her maternity leave was over. I didn't think I had a choice, so I said yes. Then I watched her and Gracie after she was born."

"How'd you end up with the Craigs?"

"Monica's mother used to take care of Haylene's grandmother. Around the time when she died, the Craigs' nanny moved out to take care of her own mother."

"Geez. Okay, keep going."

"Yeah, a lot had to happen before I got involved. The Craigs asked Monica's mom if she wanted to stay on as their nanny. She said fuck no, she was done taking care of other people's families, but Monica asked me if I was interested. I realized I could actually get paid a salary for what I was doing at home for like ten bucks a day and gas money."

"Incentive matters."

"Exactly. They liked that I was young and not likely to die or retire anytime soon and their sons thought I was a badass, so it was easy to keep them in line." Rafe picked at the edge of his cloth napkin that was still on the table. "They hired me, my grandma came to help out with Hope and Gracie, and here I am. That's my whole life story."

"Do you enjoy it? Watching other people's children," Sloan asked.

"I do. I don't know. It's never boring with kids. I liked hanging out at the shop with Hector and my uncles, but watching Hope discover her own toes and waiting for Monica to come home so I could show her that Gracie was walking was pretty cool. Watching kids experience things for the first time never gets old."

"That's funny. That's my favorite part of being a mom, aside from having two mini mes that I just want to snuggle all the time. Even when Avery says something fresh or Addison does something like trying to take apart a toaster, I'm in awe watching the way they take on the world."

"It's pretty crazy. Also, I feel like kids run into plenty of shitty adults along the way, so if I can be a good adult in their life, that has to count for something."

"It does. I—my mom and I fought a lot about her being my constant shadow, but I think about how my experience would have been if she'd just dropped me off at high school when I was seven and just walked away."

"She went to school with you?"

"Yep. Right up through med school. She sat behind me or beside me every day. For a long time, I thought she just didn't trust me."

"She didn't trust anyone with her baby."

"Sure didn't. To say I can relate is an understatement. I want to protect them all the time."

"You always will. Hope doesn't leave for college for a year and I'm already praying she picks a local school. And she's not even my kid."

"She and Gracie are lucky to have you."

"Yeah, I love those little punks."

The waitress arrived with their massive steaks and topped off their drinks. They both ate in silence for a few moments. She didn't want to get ahead of herself, but so far this was a pretty perfect first date.

"I like being with you," she confessed.

"I like being with you." Rafe reached over and took her hand, reducing Sloan to a puddle of gush and feels when he brushed his lips across her fingers. She knew it was way too soon to make the call, but she had a feeling that Rafe Whitcomb was a real keeper.

Chapter Fourteen

Something was off with Rafe when he woke up the next morning. His date with Sloan had been exactly what he'd wanted. A quiet night out, just the two of them. Good food, open and honest conversation. After he'd paid the bill, Sloan said she wanted to go to the beach. They drove to Venice and walked down the paths, away from the booths and vendors.

Rafe had looked at the lights in the distance from the pier and, for a moment, considered how much his life had changed since the first time he set foot on the same beach. He'd spent more time thinking about how good it felt to be there with Sloan under his arm. When they got back to the house, they had sex on the living room floor on top of one of the dozens of fluffy-ass blankets that Sloan kept around the house.

They'd ended up in Sloan's bed, where she fell asleep in his arms. After listening to her snore for a good hour, Rafe called it a night himself, drifting off with her soft body pressed against him. When they woke up, neither of them were in a hurry to get out of bed. Rafe would make them waffles when they got their asses in gear and made their way downstairs, but for now chilling in Sloan's bedroom and watching British cooking shows was perfectly fine by him.

For some reason, though, Rafe couldn't stop thinking about how they were running out of time. A little more than twenty-fours and they would have to get back to pretending there was nothing romantic going on between them. He actually missed the girls. The house wasn't the same without them. He missed their energy, their never-ending questions and their attempts at silly jokes, but the moment they popped into his head, all Rafe could think about was their asshole father, Drew. There was a line between what was now his business and what was for Sloan to keep to herself, but she and her kids mattered to him now in a different way and there was something about that that was just digging at him.

"I'll be right back. Tell me if I miss the judging for the tarts." Sloan hopped up and went to her closet. She came back out wearing a thin, silk night thing that made her tits look amazing before she slipped into the bathroom. Rafe grabbed the remote and hit pause. He was rooting for the young Irish kid to win the whole thing, but that didn't matter at the moment. Sloan came out of the bathroom, lotioning her hands.

"Oh, you paused it. Thank you." She flopped back down on the bed, but Rafe didn't hit play.

"Can I ask you something?"

Sloan sat up and moved, so she was facing him with her legs crossed. "Sure, what's up? Is everything okay?"

"I was wondering what happened between you and Drew"

"Like all of it or why did we split up?"

"Why did you split up, with a side of as much as you want to tell me."

"He cheated, but that was the other shoe. When we met, he had so much more professional experience. He was older, cooler. His private practice was finally doing well. I think he saw me as someone he could mold and control, and also be his arm candy. But when I refused to come work for him, he started gaslighting me. Everything I did would have been better if I'd done it with him.

"When I started pushing back, he started saying that I was selfish because I wasn't using my talents to help build his practice. It was hard enough being a very young Black woman trying to get respect in her field—that's still hard, but then to get that shit from him at home? It messed with my head a lot.

"When I got pregnant with the girls, he was...kinder, for a little while. When I was, like, six months along, he casually mentioned how happy he was that things were 'working out'. He thought, or he'd hoped, I was going to give up medicine to stay home with them, which I had no plan to do. We fought about that a lot. And when I went back to work, he strayed. To her credit, the woman he cheated with felt bad. She told me everything. I think she was trying to save our family, but I don't know—to me that was like my way out. I knew I was done. I just didn't know how to tell him that I didn't love him anymore.

"The fun part about having kids with your ex is that you can never shake them. Leaving Seattle has helped a lot. I've never been happier. The sunshine helps too, but I feel like I can breathe here and I don't have to worry about seeing him a few times a week. Now I'm just hoping he falls into a sinkhole and I never have to deal with him again."

"But he's okay with the girls?"

"Yeah, he's fine," she said, waving him off. "He loves them, in his own arrogant way. His mother does most of the parenting when they're with him. Part of the reason I didn't fight for full custody is because Susan is a good grandmother and they like being with her."

"Did he ever put his hands on you?"

"No. He didn't, but I can tell you want to beat his ass and I appreciate it. What's on your mind?"

"A couple things." Rafe reached up and let the side of his knuckle trail down her neck. Sloan leaned into his touch.

"Care to tell me?"

"I was thinking about how I feel about you."

"Yeah?"

"And I'm thinking about how hard it's going to be for me when the girls get back."

"What do you mean?"

"I'm just thinking about how long it's going to be before I accidentally touch you or fuck up, and kiss you goodnight in front of them."

"Oh. Yeah. I've been thinking about that too."

"And I'm thinking about where the line is with me and Drew."

"Yeah, that too. With him, I'll—I'll let you know. You and I are together. I just want you to worry about us. All of my feelings for Drew involve regret and time wasted. It's not a situation where I see us as this family that could have had it all if something had just been different. I can't stand his ass in a real way. But I can handle him. And I'm not saying that like I don't want you to care."

"I know."

"I just—I can handle him. But the girls are a different story."

"This is your call because they're your children, but when we go to my parents' tonight and when you meet my friends, I want to introduce you as my girlfriend. I don't want to pretend we're just friends and I sure as fuck don't want to spend the whole night telling myself I can't touch you or kiss you."

"I'd like that." Sloan leaned forward and kissed him, but the soft smile on her lips faded as fast as it appeared. "When the girls get home tomorrow, I'll talk to them. Or we can talk to them together, tell them we've initiated—" Sloan cut herself off.

"What?"

"I was going to say that we're initiating step one of the new daddy plan, but I think that might give them the wrong impression. Not to say—"

"No, I get it. We're not exactly sure where this is going, so we can't tell them it's headed that way."

Rafe hated this part of the dating game, where one or both parties held shit back, or took too much care in tiptoeing around certain things so they didn't scare the other person off. Rafe knew that what he was feeling for Sloan was intense. He also knew he could already see a future with her, but she was right. It was too soon to be talking about forever.

"We can tell them that we like each other and that we don't know what will happen, but we'll keep them in the loop. And then we can brace ourselves for fifty follow-up questions."

"Yeah, I'm pretty sure they'll steer the conversation from there." Sloan chuckled and slid her hand over his stomach. His abs tensed under her touch as a rush of warmth flooded his body. "I don't know how to explain it, but I want you. In my life."

"I feel the same way."

"Good—" Sloan's stomach let out the loudest growl.

"You hungry there, champ?"

"Apparently."

"Come on. I'll make you breakfast while we see who's gonna take home this week's star baker."

•

Rafe had never wanted to pat himself on the back harder and with more relief and satisfaction than he did after he introduced Sloan to the rest of his family. Before they left the house, he pulled up their family text stream.

> *Sloan and I are on our way.*
> *We've decided to give a relationship a try.*
> *Direct all audience questions to me.*
> *Thank you.*

Then he set his phone to Do Not Disturb and drove himself and Sloan across town to his parents' house. When they got there, Gracie was bouncing off the walls and couldn't help but mention to Sloan that she had already suggested that Rafe marry her. She was glad they were at least getting the ball rolling. After Gracie escaped from the headlock Rafe put her in, he took Sloan into the house to introduced her to his dad and Hope.

Immediately Monica put Sloan to work assembling skewers and Joe sent Rafe to help their elderly neighbor Mrs. Davis change a lightbulb in her garage. When he got back from Mrs. Davis's, both his parents shot him looks that made it clear he had an earingful coming his way, but for the time being, they just let him and Sloan enjoy the block party.

Finally they helped themselves to the first round of burgers and chicken skewers off the grill and then they joined Gracie and Hope on the porch. The neighbor's son Darius had set up his speakers on the other side of street, blasting 70's and 80's R&B classics, which had Monica two-stepping in front of the grill. BBQing with his family and neighbors, hanging out with his sisters, listening to Monica laugh with her friends—they'd been here dozens of times before, but it was different having Sloan with him this time.

Rafe felt different. He sat back, hiding the smile that wanted to plaster itself across his cheeks as he watched Sloan with Gracie and Hope talking her head off. Hope's cell phone appeared in front of Rafe's face. He leaned back and looked at a red carpet photo of a beautiful Asian woman and an average-looking White dude.

"You have to follow this site," Gracie said. "They post all of her outfits. WhatNadiWore.com."

"I love that dress," Sloan said with a dramatic sigh.

Rafe took the phone and looked closer before handing it back. "Who are these people?"

"Nadia Chau and her new husband, Prince James. They had, like, the biggest wedding of the decade. Where were you?"

"He was probably asleep," Hope said. "The wedding came on at four a.m.. You know her, Rafe. She's on *Galaxis*."

"Ah, okay," Rafe remembered her when Hope dropped the reference. She'd made him binge watch three seasons of *Galaxis* for a short story she was writing for her friends. On the show, Nadia wore a ton of make-up to make her look like an alien. He remembered the weekend they got married too. The female members of the Baker family were all about it, but he'd had that Saturday off and gone for a ride up the coast with the boys. Clearly he'd made a mistake and missed out on the wedding to end all weddings.

"I woke up to watch it," Sloan said with a chuckle. "Totally worth it."

Rafe took the phone back and looked at the photograph a little harder. "Oh okay. She looks different in this picture. Couldn't pick him out of a line up."

"I can't imagine marrying a prince," Gracie said.

"That's a hard no for me," Hope agreed. "I don't like having my picture taken like that."

"Yeah, you do!" Gracie leaned over and snapped a selfie of them both. Rafe looked up as their father came out of the house, his keys jingling in his hand. He tapped Rafe on the shoulder, then pointed to his pick-up truck parked at the curb.

"I'm gonna run and get some more ice. Come on."

Rafe stood and turned to Sloan. "The store is just around the corner. Will you be okay?"

"Yeah, I'll be fine. I've missed at least the last four months worth of Nadia's outfits. That should keep me busy."

"Dad, can you get me some Skittles?" Gracie asked.

"Oh yeah. Double the Skittles?" Hope added.

"Double the Skittles. Let's go."

The whole way to the store, his dad told him about the issues he was having with some of the guys on his crew at the airport. Aircraft maintenance was no joke. When they pulled into the parking lot, his dad put his truck in park and things took a fucking turn.

"So, she's the one?" Joe said, all casual like.

"Whoa! What the hell? It's been, like, an hour," Rafe replied. Yeah, he was falling pretty hard for Sloan, but that was his business and he didn't need his dad calling him out like that.

"And you brought her home. The last girl you let hang out with your sisters was Kelly. I've seen the way you've been looking at her all day. You can't fool me, boy. I know what it's like."

"Of course I like her. I said that last week. We're together. I want you guys to get to know her. There's a leap between all that and her being the one."

"So, it hasn't crossed your mind?"

"I—" Rafe couldn't deny it. He'd thought about all kinds of shit, including what it would mean. He'd been thinking about it ever since Avery tossed the Dad grenade. He looked out the window and scrubbed his hand through his beard. Joe went on.

"I'm gonna go out on a limb here and guess that you didn't tell her you could only stay on to the end of the year."

"No, I did not."

"So, are you staying on for her or the kids?"

Rafe sighed and pressed his head back into the headrest. "I don't know, Dad. Both? They're good kids. She's an amazing woman."

"You know you can keep dating her and not watch her kids."

"I know."

"I'm not saying you have to up and quit. I'm just thinking back to the beginning of the summer when you sat there on my couch and told me you were done. You said you wanted to move on and I know you didn't have a solid plan, but I also know you give a lot of yourself. I thought you were ready to give something else a go."

"Yeah."

"You hear me, Rafael?"

"Yes, I hear you."

"You can go back to school. You can go work for your Uncle Nick at the shop. You can still do whatever you want."

"I think I just didn't want to move to Australia. Moving on to a different family is one thing. I couldn't uproot myself and I didn't want to miss Hope's senior year."

"I'm not saying any of this because of Sloan. She's a great girl. Monica loves her and Hope took to her right away. Gracie wants to move in with her. And you know I'm never going to complain about you dating a doctor. You've just been doing a lot for other families for a long time, and yeah you were paid for it, but your time and your dreams are important too. I—I know a lot of that blame falls on me."

Rafe turned and looked at his dad. "What are you talking about? I don't blame you. What would I have to blame you for?"

"I could have made you go back to school. I coulda—"

"Dad. I fucked up. I could have gone back to school, but I chickened out."

"Yeah, well you wouldn't have been in that situation if I hadn't—"

"If you hadn't moved us out here. Yeah I know, but I don't see it that way. Do you think I wish we were back in Woburn? Cause I don't. I didn't start fucking up when we moved out here. I had just been fucking up in a familiar place with cops who didn't give a shit what White boys were doing."

"Yeah," Joe said quietly. Sure, things changed when they came to the West coast, but there wasn't some magical life Rafe was missing out on three thousand miles away. He'd tracked down old friends from his junior high school. He knew what they were up to and he knew he wasn't missing out on a damn thing. Sure as fuck, nothing he would trade Monica and his sisters for. Nothing he would trade Sloan and her girls for either.

"Stop beating yourself up," he said to his dad. "I hear you and I will tell Sloan if and when I'm ready to move on to something else. I won't spring it on her and I won't keep it all in until it turns into resentment or something worse. Do I have some shit to figure out? Yeah. But right now, this is what I want."

"Good. I just know love can make you do crazy shit sometimes."

"Like buy a lifetime supply of Brita filters?"

"Hey, you make fun, but look at my skin." Some of the redness on his dad's face had gone away. "I look forty again."

"Let's not get carried away now."

"We need bags of ice and some Skittles."

"Can't forget the Skittles. Let's go."

When they got back to the house, it was a little after sunset. Rafe spotted his uncles' cars and Eddie and Hector's bikes when he pulled in. Carrying the ice inside, he ran into Eddie and Hector in the driveway.

"Yo, we just met your girl. That's the doctor?" Eddie asked.

"Yep. Feel free to shut up about it at any time."

"Nah, man. I gotta know. How in the fuck did you land a chick like that? She's fine as hell."

"Yeah, man. She *is* fine," Hector agreed.

"Did you scare her away?" Rafe looked around the side of the house and didn't see her in the yard.

"Nah, she went inside to make a phone call."

"Cool. I'll be right back." Rafe filled the big cooler with ice, then went inside where he found Sloan pacing in the kitchen. She smiled at him, scrunching up her nose.

"I miss you too. So, so much. The house is so empty without my babies.— Yes, I'll see you so soon. — No, I have a half day tomorrow, so I'll come to the airport to pick you up. — I'll ask Rafe if he wants to come too.— Okay, I love you, love you, love you both. Goodnight." Then she ended the call and turned to him. "Hey."

Rafe sat at the table and reached for her. She came right over to him and took a seat in his lap. "How are they doing?"

"Fine. Their dad took them out on his boat today."

"Oh yeah?"

"Yeah. They had a good time, but I'm ready for them to come back. I met your friends."

" Eddie told me. Did they go easy on you?"

"They did. They're very nice. I had a chat with Monica too."

"God, what did she say."

Sloan chuckled a bit. "It was fine. She just wanted to confirm that we were actually together, as a couple. Then she told me I should be able to fire you if I've caught feelings."

Rafe shook his head. "My own mother. Damn."

"And then she said I shouldn't be ashamed not to fire you—something about women working for their husbands for decades, and stay-at-home dads being a thing, and millenial feminism. I tried to explain that we weren't quite married yet and she casually changed the subject. She did tell me to bring the girls over when I was up for it. I thought that was sweet."

"Yeah, maybe. She might be using you for placeholder grandchildren. Be on your guard. She's got a lot of pent up grandmothering in her."

"I'll keep my head on the swivel. How was your ice run?"

"Ice was secured, but mostly my dad just wanted to sing your praises in private."

"I'm sure. That was the longest twenty minutes of my life. Can I have a kiss?"

"Oh, I'll kiss you."

Rafe turned his face upward as Sloan placed her hands on either side and pressed her lips to his. It was a tame kiss, but that didn't stop the soft press of her mouth from flooding his senses. He could go on kissing her for a long, long time.

"You're cute, Dr. Copeland," he whispered against her mouth.

"Why, thank you," she whispered back before kissing him again.

"Ewww!"

He pulled away and saw Gracie standing in the door with the instant camera she'd gotten for her birthday.

"Don't you have somewhere to be?" he asked.

"I just wanted to grab my camera. I told mom I'd take some pictures for Hope's senior spread in the yearbook. Here." She handed Sloan a small instant photo. It was still developing, but by the time they heard the front door slam behind Gracie, a damn adorable picture of him and Sloan kissing came into clear view.

"You keep this," Sloan said. "The girls may know how to knock on a door, but they do not respect my privacy."

"Will do." He moved to stand and slipped the small picture into his wallet. Sloan gave his arm a little tug.

"Come on. Something tells me Eddie has all kinds of fun stories to tell about you," Sloan teased, backing out of the kitchen. Rafe groaned, but willingly followed.

Chapter Fifteen

When the mudroom door clicked shut behind them, Rafe flipped the lock and Sloan fell silent. She'd had a wonderful time with Rafe and his family, but as they drove back home there was only one thing on her mind—this would be their last full night together for a month.

After they both stepped out of their shoes, she took his hand and led him up the stairs to her bedroom. She pushed the dimmer on her overhead lights up halfway and turned to face him. She started undressing, making her intentions very clear. That dark intensity came over his eyes as he backed her toward the bed.

Sloan sunk down on the foot of the mattress and watched closely as Rafe dropped to his knees between her feet. He reached for the hem of her shirt and she did what she could to make it easy for him to pull it over her head. She took her bra off and tossed it on the floor.

In the next second, Rafe's lips were on hers. She took advantage, scooting to the corner of the mattress, dropping her arms over his shoulders as his strong, rough hands eased their way up her sides. She couldn't think straight. The only thing her mind was processing was how badly she wanted him to make her come, how badly she wanted to feel his body against hers.

They kept on kissing, their tongues moving together until Sloan could barely breathe. She could feel her panties soaking as her pussy clenched on itself. She was painfully empty, and while his fingers and his tongue worked absolute magic, she only wanted one thing. Rafe's cock buried deep inside her until she screamed.

Her eyes blinked open when Rafe pulled back just enough to meet her gaze. She felt her teeth gripping her bottom lip. They'd been all over each other all weekend and it still wasn't enough. She couldn't imagine the withdrawal she'd be going through when they couldn't be alone. But she'd worry about that another time, not when Rafe's hands were smoothing their way over her breasts. He kept focused on her eyes as he pinched her nipples lightly, before massaging them with his palms.

"Sloan, you're the only app I'm running right now."

She couldn't help the snort that came bursting out of her mouth. "You're never gonna let me forget that, are you?"

He shook his head, eyes wide, "No." Sloan's laughter melted into a moan as he pinched her nipples again, harder this time. The pressure edged near pain, but that didn't stop Sloan from leaning closer, silently begging for more. Her hand slid into his hair as his head dipped lower. He captured her nipple in his mouth, licking and sucking until she was crying out.

He switched to the other side, sliding his tongue over her left nipple as his fingers returned to the right, lightly pinching and stroking the puckered wet tip. She tugged at his short hair, while holding him closer all at once. He became less gentle then, sucking and lightly biting. She didn't realize her hips were moving until his hand slid between her legs. One brush against the fabric of her jeans was all she could handle.

"Stop, stop," she panted. Rafe immediately pulled away.

"Yes, hi."

"Please take off your clothes."

"Since you asked so nicely." Rafe stood and started to undress. Sloan followed, standing to shuck off her jeans and her underwear. She reached into her nightstand drawer and pulled out the last two condoms they had stashed there. When she turned around, the sight of his naked body was almost too much. She had to wonder when she would be able to look at his well-toned form and his sprawling tattoos, and not want to start drooling.

"Jesus, Rafe."

"What?"

"I wish you could see yourself."

"Oh, I'd much rather be looking at you. Come here."

Sloan walked into his arms, wrapping her fingers around his erection. She only stroked his perfectly thick length up and down a few times before he stilled her hand.

"Nah, hold on."

"What—" Rafe picked her up and threw her on the bed. The noise that burst out of Sloan was a mix between a screech and a hysterical laugh. Rafe crawled beside her, but before she could get hold of up or down, he was guiding her body on top of his so she was face to face with his glorious dick. His tongue was lapping over her parted pussy lips.

Sloan leaned back, digging her knees into the covers, pressing herself back against the wet suction of his mouth. She eased forward and back until she was reminded of the dripping cock in front of her as it brushed against her cheek. She took his erection between her lips, sucking him as far down as she could. Her fingers stroked the inches she couldn't fit in her mouth.

They found a perfect rhythm that had Sloan shamelessly riding Rafe's face until she was coming. She let his dick slip out of her mouth and she pressed her forehead against his thigh. She came again. It felt like forever between when she stopped trembling and when she could finally register the soft kisses that Rafe was spreading all over her skin. Sloan followed the gentle movement of his hands as he moved her off of him and onto her side of the bed. She could still barely breathe when he climbed back over her, this time with a condom sheathed over his cock.

He kissed the side of her face, then her cheeks and her lips. She could taste herself on him and that just made her ready for more. His lips moved over her cheek again and his hand gripped her asscheek nice and hard. Sloan arched into his grip, letting out a pathetic moan.

"Tell me how you want it," he whispered.

Sloan leaned up and kissed him on the lips before she rolled onto her stomach. "I want you on top of me."

Rafe gave her exactly what she wanted and better than she'd imagined. He moved over her, trapping her thighs between his, pushing her legs together. The pressure squeezed her clit against her swollen, wet lips. With his hand under her hip, he guided her ass up in the air, giving him just enough room to push his cock in nice and deep.

He moved slowly, dragging his lips over her shoulder as he pumped in and out. Sloan felt weightless, sinking into her sheets. Every pleasure point in her body seemed focused between her legs. Before she realized it, Rafe had become completely still. Sloan was the one doing the moving, fucking herself slow, but hard on his dick, thighs clamped shut, creating the sweetest pressure.

His lips brushed over her ear. The light touch made her pussy clench around him. "Does that feel good?" he groaned.

"Mhmm," was all she could manage, but just admitting it to him, to herself, out loud was enough. She realized then that she'd been holding back with him. Call it the new boyfriend jitters, but now she knew she didn't have to. She had no clue when it had happened, but she could feel a palpable change. She didn't have to guard herself, worry about what he might say, or what he might think. With him, she felt safe, free to show him exactly what she wanted and *how* she really wanted it.

She let go, soaking up the warmth of his body pressed on top of her and the strokes of his mouth over her skin. She could feel herself on the edge of blacking out from pure pleasure when she arched off the bed, pushing Rafe's dick out as she squirted all over her sheets. He thrust back inside, sending another tremor through her whole body. Somehow, her body was still craving more. She fucked herself on him more, harder, rougher, until she squirted again. Somewhere in the distance, in the haze of her pulsing orgasm, she heard Rafe let out the sexiest groan. She couldn't possibly want more, but she did.

Rafe collapsed on the bed beside her. When Sloan's eyes finally opened, he reached up and stroked her cheek.

"Did you come?" she asked.

Rafe frowned. "Did I come? If we were less responsible, you'd definitely be pregnant."

"Oh, well good thing we were careful."

Rafe didn't say anything, he just winked at her. In the few long moments they lay together in silence, there were things she wanted to tell him. Things she wanted to say, sweet things, romantic things, but she kept those confessions to herself. She'd tell him one day, though. Maybe sometime soon. Deep down, she knew there was no stopping it. But for now, she would have to settle for closing the distance between her and her boyfriend, and kissing him on his perfect, soft lips.

•

Sloan was extra on edge, but hopefully things would be somewhat sorted out in a few hours. After they got the girls dinner, she and Rafe were going to sit them down and tell them that they had started seeing each other. Sloan may have googled "how to tell your kids you're dating again" earlier that morning. The constant takeaway was transparency, honesty and listening with an open heart to how your kids were taking the news.

She suspected they would be on board, but she didn't want to confuse them and she didn't want to pressure them into accepting something they weren't ready for quite yet. She was also anxious to see them. She missed her babies. It didn't help that she couldn't hold Rafe's hand while they were waiting for Addison and Avery in the Alaskan Airlines baggage terminal. She could feel him next to her—a tall, buff ball of his own nervous energy. She almost reached over and looped her arm through his, but caught herself at the last minute.

"I can't believe you baked that many cookies." She'd come home early from her second consult to find Rafe standing in the kitchen, a sweets factory worth of snickerdoodles cooling on the island.

"I don't know, I couldn't sit still. I figure they can bring the leftover four dozen cookies into school tomorrow and you can bring some into the medical center. Have a full on bake sale at one of the nurses' stations."

"Ehhh, I don't know if I want to set a baked goods precedent. Unless you wanna keep baking for the medical center staff."

"I'll get back to you on that."

"Yeah, that's what I thought."

"I washed your sheets and made your bed."

"Oh, thank you." Sloan checked her smart watch. Their flight was on time. "I have no idea which door they're coming out of."

"They've been doing construction here for, like, ten years. Give them thirty or so more and I think they'll have it right."

"I should have brought balloons," she nudged Rafe and nodded to the two teen girls a few feet away carrying what looked like fifty balloons and a sign for "Jessica". They were too busy filming each other on their phones to notice that they were getting a few looks themselves.

"Balloons and stuffed animals next time," Rafe teased.

"Oh, I'll be mom of the year." Just then, another teen girl came out of a doorway off to the left. She immediately started screaming and running toward her friends. Sloan smiled for less than half a second, before her stomach dropped to the floor. She heard one of her girls absolutely wailing before she could even see her. Sloan was already halfway across the baggage area before she realized she was moving. Avery came through the departure tunnel door first. She was tugging Drew behind her. He had a firm grip on Addison with his other hand. Tears were streaming down her face too, but she was silent.

"What the hell?" she said under her breath. "Come here, baby."

Drew let Avery go and she sprinted into Sloan's arms. Sloan wiped her face, then looked her over for any apparent injuries. She looked up at her ex-husband. Horrible things didn't happen in slow motion, they happened fast. So fast that it would take Sloan a while to really process the whole scene. She felt Rafe behind her. Heard Addison say his name as she reached for him with her free hand, but Drew wouldn't let her go.

"You son of bitch," Drew seethed. And then he let go of Addison and lunged for Rafe. Sloan narrowly missed taking a knee to the face as she pulled Avery out of the way. Rafe had the reflexes to dodge the first punch Drew threw. Drew stumbled a half step, but quickly spun around and tried to punch Rafe again. This time, Rafe caught him and put him in a body hold, straining both of Drew's arms behind his back.

"I don't know what your problem is, but you need to relax. Right now," Rafe said just loud enough for Sloan to hear. Both girls were in her arms, trembling and crying. Drew was looking right at them, but it didn't seem to matter. He threw his head back, trying to headbutt Rafe in the nose. He missed again.

"You think you can come in," Drew said, "and try to take my fucking kids. Try and take my fucking wife."

"Drew! Stop!" Sloan heard herself say, but she could tell nothing she said would stop him. She'd never seen Drew like this before, blood red in the face, nearly foaming at the mouth. He kept struggling against Rafe's iron hold like he was willing to hurt himself just to hurt Rafe. She had no idea what would get him to stop. Until the airport police showed up.

•

Sloan was perfectly still, but inside she felt like every inch of her was quaking. As soon as Rafe saw the officers, he let Drew go, but it took all three cops to get Drew to finally settle down. He thoroughly scared the shit out of the girls who were currently clinging to Sloan, even though their tears has stopped.

It had taken a few tries, but Sloan was sure she had the gist of the story. Drew had told the girls that he wanted them to move back to Seattle to live with him permanently. When they'd refused, he made a comment about them liking Rafe more than him. Sloan could just hear his tone, backhanded and condescending. Avery told him that was in fact the case and that soon Rafe would be their new daddy, and they wouldn't need to visit Drew at all. Drew demanded clarification and the girls had some for him. Addison had seen Rafe and Mommy kiss and that meant that Rafe liked Mommy and Mommy liked Rafe.

Sloan could only picture how Drew had flown off the handle. It was bad enough that he was so pissed that he got on a plane. Sloan tried not to picture what would have happened if Rafe had shown up to the airport to get the girls by himself. Or worse, if Drew had shown up at the house.

Two older women and a man a little older than Sloan had come to check on them, asking if they were okay. The three teen girls stayed and one of them had recorded the whole thing. One of the women was still hanging around with her husband. They didn't say anything else, but Sloan appreciated the silent support.

The officers took Drew somewhere and separated her and Rafe in the terminal so they could question them both. They were done speaking with Sloan, but two cops were still talking to Rafe a few baggage carousels away.

"Mommy, did we get Rafe in trouble with daddy and the police?" Avery asked.

"No, baby. You didn't at all. Your daddy made a bad choice and did a bad thing. You are not responsible for that."

Sloan looked up as one of the cops who had just been speaking to Rafe approached her. "Mrs. Copeland. We have your husband—"

"Ex-husband and it's Dr. Copeland."

"I'm sorry. Dr. Copeland. Would you like to press charges?"

"That's not up to me. He attacked my friend, not me."

"Mr. Whitcomb believes that Mr. Ballos isn't a threat to him. He said that would be up to you."

"I—I might have to. He's not even supposed to be here. They usually fly unaccompanied."

"We'll hold him for a few hours and then put him back on a plane to Seattle." Sloan was reminded then that it was almost Tuesday. There was no way Drew didn't have patients in the morning. How could he have been so stupid. Reckless rage caused you to do stupid things, apparently.

"I might have to file a restraining order."

"That might not be a bad idea."

Finally, the officers exchanged four different head nods, then let Rafe go. He came right back to them and Addison ran into his arms. He scooped her up and hugged her close. "We can go."

Just then, one of the teen girls came rushing over to them. "Hi. Sorry, we recorded the whole thing. Me and my friend, you know, just in case the cops got out of hand."

"Thank you," Sloan said, fighting back tears. Sloan could easily picture how much worse the situation could have gotten.

"We can email you the videos. Just in case you need them for, like, legal purposes or whatever."

Rafe looked at Sloan. "That's not a bad idea."

The girl waved over her friends and the three of them sent her all the footage they had. She thanked them and the couple who had hung around just in case, and then finally all parties went their own way.

"We're gonna go home now, okay?" Sloan told the girls as they walked to short-term parking. After they got them settled in their car seats, Sloan caught Rafe's eye as they both moved toward the front of the car. He looked at her over the hood.

"Are you okay?" he asked.

"Not at all. You?"

"Nope. You find out what set him off?"

Sloan didn't want to make Rafe even more upset, but he needed to know everything. "Addison saw us kissing. She might have seen more."

The color drained out of Rafe's face. "And she told him."

"Yup. I'll tell you the rest later."

"Yeah, okay." They climbed in the car and Sloan immediately turned and leaned between their seats. She wiggled Addison's foot.

"You okay, my love bugs?"

"Yeah, we're okay. I did see you kiss. I didn't mean to, but I saw it," Addison said. Sloan knew that tone and her heart broke. At some point during this whole ordeal, Drew had called her a liar.

Sloan was hoping to get them home and fed, but apparently they were having this conversation now. Rafe knew it too. He turned in his seat to face the girls.

"We didn't mean for you to see that, sweetie," Sloan said. "That was a mistake."

Avery threw up her hands. "I don't get it. If Rafe can't be our daddy, then why were you kissing?"

Well, she'd failed the honesty portion and the whole not confusing your kid part too. Sloan might as well come clean.

"Sometimes adults aren't sure what they want. When you asked if Rafe could be your daddy, we weren't sure if we were more than friends yet and we didn't want to tell you until we knew."

"Do you know now?" Avery asked.

Sloan glanced at Rafe. His stressed look matched hers.

"Yeah, we do. Rafe's my boyfriend now."

"And I'm still your nanny."

"That's right. He's still going to take care of you. That won't change. But we just aren't at the daddy phase of things yet, okay babies? We're still getting to know each other and it takes time before two people decide to get married. Does that make sense?"

"Yes," Avery said. Addison just nodded.

"We messed up and we're sorry," Rafe said.

"And it's okay if you don't want to forgive us right now," Sloan added. "We made things confusing for you and your dad didn't make things any better."

"I hate him," Addison said. Tears started welling in her eyes again.

"Daddy said Addison was bullshit. And then he said he was gonna get Rafe fired and make us live with him."

"Please don't make us go back. I don't want to go back," Addison said, the tears flowing freely again. Sloan's heart split in two when Avery reached over and started wiping her sister's cheeks. Sloan was gonna kill Drew.

"You won't have to," she said. "I promise."

Chapter Sixteen

After a quick trip to the McDonald's drive-thru to ease the tension with nuggets and Happy Meal toys, they took the girls straight home. They were pretty jazzed to see the mountain of cinnamon sugar cookies waiting for them, but they were only momentarily distracted. They had more questions about their dad and what was going to happen next. Sloan told them the truth. She didn't know, but she would handle it.

She tried to distract them, asking more questions about the Under the Sea unit they would be continuing this week with Mrs. Brown. By the time they finished their dinner, Sloan could tell they were completely wrung out. Aside from the shit **Drew** had just pulled, they'd been running around since Friday. They had to be exhausted.

"Why don't we do bath time a little early and then we can just veg out and watch a movie. How does that sound?"

Avery hopped off her stool "Yeah, okay." Addison didn't say anything. She just followed, her eyes down.

"Do you mind?" she asked Rafe. "I'm gonna call my mom."

"Yeah, sure. Take as much time as you need." He kissed her on the forehead and followed the girls upstairs.

Her mom was just about to leave her sister's house for the night when she answered. She put the call on speaker, and Sloan told them both everything. She managed to hold back the tears, but as she recounted the whole incident at the airport, she started shaking. The adrenaline in her system wasn't quite done with her yet.

"I might have to challenge his custody, Mom. I can't—this can't happen again and I definitely don't want to risk something even worse happening."

"Well, you know how I felt when you left him. There are mistakes and there are major red flags. This a red flag the size of a football field—"

"And you know what comes after a red flag?" Lauryn suddenly said into the phone. "An ejection. Kick him all the way to the curb, girl."

Sloan burst out laughing. A few tears came with it. "I think you're talking about a red card. But thanks, Laur."

"Same thing. What would you tell me if Pres pulled something like that?" Lauryn's husband was the sweetest man. Sloan couldn't even imagine him raising his voice in anger at her sister, let alone their son.

"I'd tell you to shove him into a cannon and aim it directly at the surface of the sun."

"Exactly."

"I want you to be happy, but more importantly I want you and the girls to be safe," her mom said. "If Drew can't control his temper, then keeping the girls away from him might be for the best."

"I just—I can't wrap my mind around it. He's always been arrogant, but he completely lost it. And I can't tell Addison that she needs to forgive him for the way he talked to her."

"Especially if there's a chance he doesn't think he did anything wrong," her mom said. "Yeah. Do you want me to come out? He got off easy with me last time. He hasn't met the full wrath of Pauletta yet."

For a moment she considered it. She hadn't seen her family in months. "No, I think we're okay for now. I'm just so pissed. Screw him."

"Let me know how me and your dad can help. And let me know when you call Wendy." Contacting her lawyer was next on Sloan's to-do list.

"I will."

"So, you're seeing this Rafe now?"

Sloan cringed. "Yeah, I know we didn't meet under ideal circumstances, but I really care about him and he's so good to the girls."

"He cute?"

"Lauryn," her mom scolded.

"Yes, he is cute and that definitely doesn't matter."

"What? I just wanted to know."

Sloan heard her mom suck her teeth. "I met your father when he was cussing out my brother for not tipping enough and that turned out fine. I've talked to Rafe a few times and he seems very nice. I'm going to talk to him again though."

"Okay," Sloan agreed.

"Dang, I want to talk to him too," Lauryn said. "I didn't meet Drew until you were engaged."

"I'll arrange a conference call." She was only half joking. She knew her dad would want in on this too.

She almost bit a hole in her bottom lip and let out a trembling breath through her nose. This was her mom's own subtle "I told you so". There was nothing bitter about it left between her and her mom anymore, but when Sloan met Drew, she and her mom were still healing from being glued together at the hip for more years than either of them liked. Her mom wanted to do things a certain way, meet his parents and all of that, but Sloan was so sick of her mother's hovering that she begged her to let her do this one thing alone.

Sloan didn't realize at the time that she was going along with what Drew wanted. Her mom wasn't going to let that happen again, even if Sloan was really grown this time. And this time, Sloan knew she was right. She trusted Rafe, but she was that level of sprung, so it would be a bad call to not to listen to her family, who wanted the best for her and her daughters.

Plus, she'd already met his family and she didn't doubt for one second that Monica was doing more than being friendly when she'd welcomed Sloan into her home. She wanted to make sure Sloan was what she and Joe wanted for Rafe. Sloan was sure they wouldn't be psyched to find out that her ex-husband had attacked their son in the middle of LAX.

Another thing to do. Apologize to the Whitcombs from bringing this drama into Rafe's life.

"I'm going to go check on the girls, but I'll call you tomorrow."

"Okay, baby. You can call back tonight if you need to. It's okay if you wake me up."

"Thanks, Mom." She knew she shouldn't blame herself for **Drew** actions, but now she couldn't help feeling like a burden to a multitude of people.

After they ended their call, Sloan opened her **LetsChat** app and saw a bunch of notifications from the group chat with the girls. Meegan was currently in a Target dressing room, snapping pictures of every outfit she was trying on. Sloan almost started typing, but she didn't want to disrupt the easy fun of their conversation. Instead she texted Xeni privately, telling her what had happened. Xeni was with her family, so she couldn't talk on the phone, but she was texting back with a fury.

You know I'm going to kill him right?
I'm not even letting the aunts handle this.
I'm gonna fuck him up myself.

Sloan smiled at her screen. Okay, maybe burden was the wrong word. She was lucky so many people had her back.

Nothing physical. I don't want you to get arrested.
But I might take you up on that hex.

Done. I'm gonna hex the shit out of him.
Also. What happens to a surgeon when they
break one of their hands in a fist fight?

"Oh my god," Sloan said out loud. "That motherf—"

They might find it hard to do the work
that pays for the children
they claim to want full custody of.

That. Take that to your lawyer.

Sloan hopped up and grabbed her laptop. She immediately pulled up the videos the young girls had sent her from the airport. She replied to Riley_Anne03 and yuriXviktor2k4ever@memail with a heartfelt thank you, then pressed play on the first video, with the volume on low. Somehow it was worse than she remembered. From where Riley and her friends were standing, they really did capture everything. Drew looked completely deranged and it was clear how hard Rafe had tried to deescalate the situation.

Sloan attached the file to a new email then started typing.

•

It was more than two hours after Rafe and the girls had headed up for their bath by the time Sloan felt like she had done all that she could do. Rage was a funny thing. It clearly made Drew lose his ever loving mind. It made Sloan sharper. Drew might never fully regret the day he lost his shit in front of their kids, but maybe finally he'd understand that Sloan meant what she said. She wasn't under his thumb and he wouldn't fuck with her life or her kids anymore.

Heartened by her own resolve and Xeni's clear thinking, Sloan headed upstairs to see how things were coming along. Addison and Avery rarely missed out on the chance to rewatch one of their Disney favorites. It was quiet and when she poked her head into the girls' bedroom, she saw that Addison was already sound asleep.

Rafe sat on the floor in between their beds, intently reading a copy of *Madeline's Rescue* in the dim light coming from Avery's unicorn lamp. Avery was laying on the floor beside him, half heartedly playing a match game on the tablet. Rafe looked up at her, the corner of his mouth tipping up. Sloan gave him a little smile back, then squatted down beside Avery. She lightly touched the back of her head, over her silk bonnet. Her hair was damp.

"Hey, baby. Do you want to get in your bed?"

"Yeah, okay." Avery closed out of the game and sat up. "I'm pretty tired."

"Come on." She let Sloan scoop her up and tuck her under the covers. "I love you," she whispered.

"I love you, too. Did you eat all the cookies?"

"No," Sloan laughed quietly. "There are plenty of cookies left."

She and Rafe said goodnight, then stepped back into the hallway.

"How was bath time?" she asked.

"Fine. Their table mate Seth has a birthday tomorrow. We just talked about that and his party this weekend. And then I showed them cute animal videos until Addison couldn't stand the cuteness anymore."

"God, I'm gonna have to buy them a pony for their birthday."

"It's a possibility," Rafe said.

"Did they let you wash their hair?"

"No. I didn't do the whole routine. I just did a co-wash or whatever and detangled it as much as they would let me. Tomorrow is basic pigtail day. I'll fancy it up with some ribbons."

"That's great. Thank you."

Rafe just nodded, a muscle in his cheek tensing. "Let's go downstairs."

"Yeah, okay," Sloan said, suddenly nervous about whatever would happen when they got down there.

Rafe flopped on the couch and let out one hell of a sigh, stretching his long legs beside her. She felt like she could fight a bear after sending that final email, but she'd only done what she could for herself and her kids. Rafe was probably in a different head space.

"How you feeling?" she asked tentatively.

"Still pretty fucked up, to be honest. Did you talk to your mom?"

"Yeah. She has my back, whatever I decide. I told her about us, of course. She wants to talk to you at some point. About us."

"Yeah, that makes sense." He closed his eyes and pushed his head back into the cushions. He'd seemed so peaceful reading that children's book and now Sloan could feel the tension rolling off of him.

Sloan wanted him to say something, anything, but she'd spent the last three hours processing and ranting while Rafe had been taking care of her kids. He needed that chance now. So Sloan sat there and waited.

"Can I be honest with you?" he said suddenly.

"Yeah, of course."

"If no one else had been there, I would have fucked him up. He wouldn't be walking right now." Rafe didn't lift his head, but he opened his eyes and looked at her. "I'm proud of myself for keeping cool, though. For his sake and mine."

"I am too. Things would have been a hundred times worse if you'd stooped to his level of BS."

Rafe's throat contracted and he closed his eyes again. He let out another deep breath and sat forward. Sloan kept her eyes on him as he scrubbed his hands through his hair, then scratched his beard.

"I wouldn't do another minute as a guest of the county for someone like him, but I was this close to doing it for you and the girls," he said, blunt and to the point. "And I'm trying to figure out if that scares me."

A massive knot tied itself in Sloan's throat. She knew any man who thought she and her kids weren't worth fighting for was not the man for her, but this was different and Rafe knew it. There was flexing, bravado, words exchanged between men and then there were the two different sides of the violence coin. Drew had picked his side and Rafe was making it clear what his side meant to him. It meant approaching a situation with a level head and choosing to be the better person, no matter how badly he wanted to prove a very specific point. Rafe knew the consequences though. He'd gotten a real, no-fucking-around taste of the consequences. Drew didn't know how lucky he was, on a lot of levels.

Sloan wiped her face, catching a tear that suddenly jumped out. Their honeymoon period was definitely over.

Rafe scratched the back of his neck, like a nervous twitch. He had to touch some part of his body before he spoke again. "When the Bakers left for Australia, I was going to give up this work for good. I was done nannying. That's why I was available when Sarah Kato called me. I was going to do something else."

The knot in Sloan's throat tightened and started to migrate south. "Oh. What were you going to do?"

"No fucking idea."

Sloan couldn't hold back her burst of laughter. That was not what she expected to hear. "Well then."

"I felt like my life had stalled out and taking that feeling across the ocean didn't seem like a great idea."

"And now? I bet being six thousand miles away from this mess sounds amazing."

Rafe shook his head. "Monica always told me that this is a job. These are not your families. But the moment I met you and Addison and Avery, something felt different. I kept telling myself it was because you weren't married and in some antiquated, bullshit way, I was filling those shoes. I know that sounds fucked and presumptuous as hell."

"No, it—"

"I kept telling myself that I was just thinking about how much I wanted you, that I wanted you so bad I wasn't thinking straight. But that wasn't it. It was you. You are beautiful, Sloan, but you are so damn smart, and kind, and full of heart and you're a good mother. You're not afraid to show people that you're a great fucking surgeon.

"That snorting laugh thing you do cracks me up. And trust me, I've been around plenty of kids I can't stand and have taken great care of them. I adore Addison and Avery. And I love how much of you I see in them. If you told me to get lost, I would, but I would always think of you guys. I'd always worry about you. I feel like—I feel like you've invited me to be a part of your family—"

"We have," Sloan said.

"No. It's more than that. I don't know how else to say this, so I'm just going to say it. I feel like you're mine." He finally looked into her eyes. "Not in a possessive, fucked up way. I feel like you've taken up this space in my heart that's just getting bigger and bigger. I feel like the fucking Grinch after he gave in to Christmas."

Sloan laughed, more tears running down her face. "I know exactly how you feel."

"I'm not going anywhere."

"I keep telling myself 'what if this', 'what if that', but that's just me being anxious about hypothetical crap that can't happen because we've already crossed those bridges. What if the girls find out? What if Drew is a complete asshole about the whole situation? What if I fall for you? All of that has already happened and all I'm left with is what is.

"I'm glad the girls have you. They love you. You make them happy. They trust you as a friend and a responsible adult. And I—I have fallen for you so hard." Sloan couldn't bring herself to say the words. She didn't know what jerk had told all of humankind that there was some sort of time limit on love, that there was a ninety-day review with matters of the heart, but she couldn't help how she felt. She was falling in love with Rafe and she did not want him to go. Maybe it was selfish, but it was how she felt.

"Then that's enough for me. How can I help with the Drew situation?" Rafe asked.

"Just help me keep things normal for the girls, their routine and everything. Not that I think you would, but don't shit-talk him in front of them. I want them to process their own feelings how they need to. I don't want to pile on."

"Done. Is there anything I could do for you?"

"Tonight? No. I've set the proper dogs on him. I'm going to talk to my lawyer about stripping his custody rights and maybe getting a restraining order. I need to hydrate and sleep. As much fun as I had today, I still need to do my job, bright and early tomorrow morning."

"Well, I'm going to go clean out the girls' overnight bags and throw in some laundry. And then I might go for a ride. I need some air."

"Okay."

"Come here." Rafe stood and pulled Sloan into his arms. He hugged her for a long time before letting her go. She went up to her room to take a shower and when she got out, there was a text from Rafe.

I'll be back.

She replied even though she had a feeling he wouldn't read it right away. She could hear his bike's engine revving in the driveway.

Ride safe.

A half hour or so later, Rafe still wasn't back. Sloan was fading. She knew she should go to sleep, but part of her wanted to make sure Rafe got home okay. She lay in the dark, staring blankly at another episode of *Golden Girls*, in the middle of her freshly washed sheets. The scent of his sunscreen and the sex they'd had were long gone. Her friends were still at it, lighting up the group chat, but she still felt too raw to have a group conversation about what had gone down.

Her phone started vibrating on her nightstand. She figured it was Xeni, checking in and ready to dish about how her mom and her aunts had driven her up the wall. She looked at the screen and wasn't entirely sure she wasn't the one who had been hexed.

She hit accept.

"Guessing you made it back to SEA-TAC okay. What do you want?"

"I just want to know if it's true," Drew said in that shit-eating tone. Sloan knew what was coming next, but she was too tired to run from it.

"If what's true?"

"Are you fucking him?"

"Does it matter? Whether you believe me or not, you took whatever you thought out on our kids."

"I was fucking shocked. Can you blame me?"

"Yeah, I can. You're a fucking adult, Drew. I have no idea why you can't act like it. What if you had punched him? What if you had broken your hand? Then what?"

"If you had a six-year-old tell you I was fucking someone else, you'd be pissed too."

Sloan scoffed, remembering the day Dara Lindsey had been waiting for her in the hospital parking garage. How she'd saved texts and emails and pictures. A lot of pictures. Sloan had thanked her, calmly driven home and ended her marriage. The girls were young, but old enough to understand what bad shouting meant and how much it scared them. They'd only heard their dad raise his voice.

"Actually, no. I wouldn't because we aren't together anymore and I don't give a damn about what you do with your personal time."

"So the answer is yes." Drew let out a disgusted laugh. "That bad boy with a bike and tats crap is your thing now? Decided to go slumming? Teach me a lesson?"

"I'm not doing this with you. I refuse. You're not going to turn me into that woman who has a man in her life who can't control himself. You've pissed me off for the last time, Drew. You've betrayed my trust and now I'm afraid of what you might do if you don't get your way. I don't think you know how unchill that is. You can be upset that the girls don't want to live with you, but you cannot assault someone because you think they've taken your place."

"I don't give a shit—" he started to shout, but then he stopped himself. Sloan closed her eyes. He'd almost let one of the most horrible things he'd ever said to her in his life slip again. The one thing that had given her the custody agreement they had now. He didn't give a shit about the girls. Sloan thought things had changed once they were born. He'd tried to be a good father to them. Gave them everything, bragged about them, but Sloan knew deep down inside, he never wanted them.

In his mind, they were the one thing that would convince Sloan to give up her career and give him back the title of the best surgeon in Seattle. But that panned out differently, hadn't it? He didn't want the girls to move in with him. He wanted to use them to drag Sloan back to Seattle. Too bad that shit was just not going to happen.

"I get it," Sloan said, swallowing down her emotions. "Your issue is with me and even if I thought for one second that you had the right to be jealous, you screwed up by taking it out on Addison and Avery. You don't have the right to my heart anymore."

"So what, Sloan? What are you saying?"

"I'm saying don't call me anymore. You're going to wait until you hear from me or my lawyer again. I'm saying that you might not see the girls again until they want to see you and until I trust you with them again. And that might not happen."

"The hell it won't."

"Goodbye, Drew." Sloan hit the end button and tossed her phone across her bed.

Chapter Seventeen

Rafe was exhausted, but he was still too amped up to sleep. His ride helped, and so did the unplanned trip to his parents' house. When he'd pulled up at the curb, he sent his dad a text letting him know he was outside and that he needed to talk. His dad didn't ask any questions. Just walked outside a few moments later in his old beat-up robe. Rafe told him what had happened, told him how close he'd coming to breaking Drew Ballos in half.

He'd even showed him the video that Sloan had forwarded to him, just in case. Rafe knew he'd done the right thing, but it meant a lot when Joe said he was proud of him. When Joe asked him if this changed how he felt about Sloan and their arrangement, Rafe told the truth—not one bit. He only regretted not giving Sloan a proper kiss goodbye before he'd taken off and told himself he'd apologize and make up for it when they grabbed a few moments alone again.

Before Rafe had headed back to the house, Joe reminded him of one crucial fact. Whatever happened between him and Sloan, blended families were complicated and unique. They came with extra care, understanding and patience. He'd been honest with Monica about how much he felt like he was fucking up as a father and that made it much easier for Monica to understand the way Rafe was feeling when he got out of juvie.

Rafe had thought back to the conversations he and Monica had had when they first met, how kind she'd been and how she'd layed out her own boundaries with father and son. It wasn't an easy transition, but Rafe wouldn't have changed a thing about it. He loved his step-mom and his sisters, and he loved his father for growing and trying to be a better man.

Would he have liked more time to enjoy the carefree, light-hearted, getting-to-know-you period with Sloan? Hell yeah, but this was the reality of the situation. Sloan came with an asshole ex-husband and Rafe was just going to have to deal with it. After he and his dad hugged it out, he'd climbed back on his bike, but he still wasn't ready to head home.

He'd rode around for another hour, winding his way back across town, minding the speed limit 'cause the last thing he needed was to wreck. He thought he'd be out cold the minute he got in his bed, but something was still eating at him and he knew he just had to accept it.

He still wanted to beat the everloving shit out of Drew and there was nothing he could do about it. He also didn't know how long he would be pissed off about the incident at the airport. He didn't know how long it would take for him to fully accept that as long as he was with Sloan and as long as he was taking care of Addison and Avery, Drew was a factor.

Rafe gave up trying to sleep and turned his TV back on. Just as he decided on some *Ink Masters* spin off, he heard a tap on his door. He hopped up and found Addison and Avery standing in the hallway. He squatted down to their level.

"Hey, what's up?"

"We heard your motorcycle. We thought you left," Avery said.

"I left for a little bit, but I just went to go see my dad. But, see? I'm back."

"Are you staying?"

"Yeah. I'm not going anywhere."

The twins were quiet for a few moments, but Rafe knew they both had more on their minds. Addison glanced at Avery, probably deciding which one of them would tell the other reason they wanted to talk to him in the middle of the night. Addison went for it.

"Do you love Mommy?" she whispered, maybe so Sloan wouldn't hear her upstairs.

"She's very special to me."

"Do you love us?" Avery asked, her tone cheery and a little louder, like she already knew the answer.

"Are you kidding me? I'm crazy about you two. But let's talk more about this during daylight hours. Let's get you back in bed."

"We can't sleep."

"Oh yeah? I was having trouble sleeping too."

"Do you know what would make me sleepy?" Avery said. That scheming look crept back in her eye. Rafe tried not to laugh.

"What's that?"

"A cookie."

Rafe shook his head, matching her expression. "No."

Avery shot him a brutal side eye, but she let it go.

"Come on," Rafe ushered them into the hallway and back upstairs, then he tucked them into bed and hugged them both.

"Rafe," Addison whispered, just as he stood from her bed. He crouched back down.

"Yeah, kiddo."

"I'm sorry Daddy was mean to you."

"You know what, I appreciate you saying that 'cause that shows me you care about me. And that means a lot to me because I care about you too. But you don't have to apologize for him, okay? None of this is your fault."

"Okay."

Back downstairs, Rafe thought maybe sleep wouldn't be so impossible this time. But first, he grabbed a cookie.

•

Life doesn't stop for ex-husband related bullshit, so the next morning, things had to go as planned. Sloan had two surgeries scheduled, the girls would be giving the Girls Scouts a try later in the week, Gracie was cheering at her first Varsity Football game on Friday night, and Addison and Avery had to put in an appearance at Seth Rosenthal's birthday party on Saturday. None of that could be put on hold just because Drew decided to lose his fucking mind. Rafe packed up the girls and two dozen snickerdoodles, and carted them off to school.

When he dropped the girls at Mrs. Brown's classroom, their teacher pulled him aside for a quick conversation, confirming the contents of the email she'd received from Sloan. The main office had been put on notice about Drew. Rafe had a feeling that Drew wouldn't show up back in L.A. unannounced at this point, but anything was possible. On his way out, Xeni waved him across the hall. He sidestepped a cluster of small children and made his way over.

"My girl okay?"

"Little rattled still, but I think she'll be okay."

"You okay?" she asked.

"Yeah, I'm fine."

"Thank you for having her back."

"Wouldn't have it any other way."

"And don't worry about Drew. I put a hex on him."

"Oh really?" Rafe laughed.

Xeni just nodded, her expression solemn. For some reason, he had a feeling her homegrown witchcraft might do the trick.

The rest of the day was a fucking slog. He hit the gym with about twenty-five percent of his usual effort. His attempt at a short nap before he made himself some lunch was a complete fail. While he was getting an easy after-school craft project for the girls together, Sloan's lawyer called.

By the time they were done talking, he had to go get Addison and Avery from school. There was an argument over the tablet after dinner, but the rest of the day had gone pretty smoothly. He tried to wait up for Sloan, who was operating into the night, but when he woke up on the couch at three a.m. with a throw blanket draped over him, he knew he'd missed her.

Wednesday was another busy day. Sloan was home in time for dinner, but she was so exhausted she threw in the towel right after she put the girls to bed.

"Are we okay?" Rafe asked as they stood in the hallway.

"Yeah. Between work and waiting to hear back from my lawyer I'm just—I don't feel like myself. I put Drew's number on Do Not Disturb, but he keeps calling and texting me."

"Did you you share that with your lawyer too?"

"I did."

"Good."

"His mom called me today too and left me this long, rambling voicemail asking me to forgive him, but I didn't call her back. Maybe I'll call her this weekend. Listen, I'd love to—"

"No, I get it. Get some sleep."

"Thanks. I want to talk some more, but I'm just wrecked and I have a valve replacement first thing in the morning."

"Get some sleep, Dr. Copeland." Sloan offered him a tight smile and a light kiss, then went to her bedroom.

Thursday night, Rafe took the girls to their first Daisy meeting. Overall, it was success, but after he put them to sleep, he decided not to wait up.

Friday, they did their hand-off at six p.m..

"So, we'll see you Sunday?" Sloan asked as he slipped on his boots in the mudroom. He had just enough time to stop for a bite to eat and then head to the high school.

"Yeah, I'll be back Sunday night. Seth's presents are already wrapped. Top shelf, hall closet. Addison kept eyeing the LEGO set I got him."

"Thank you. You're a lifesaver."

Rafe stood and kissed Sloan on the cheek.

"I'll see you later."

"Bye."

After the game, the plan was to meet up with Hector and Eddie, but when Rafe climbed back on his bike in the high school lot, he just wasn't feeling the idea of a boys' night. He headed back to Sloan's place, making two stops in search of a suitable bouquet of flowers. Grocery store roses were the best he could manage. When he got back to the house, he found Sloan watching TV in bed, doing something on her laptop.

"Hey," she said, perking up. For the first time all week, she looked happy to see him. "How was the game?"

"It was good. Home team won and Gracie cheered her ass off. These are for you." He knelt beside the bed on the floor, handing her the flowers.

She pressed them against her nose before she smiled back him, her grin a little wider. "Thank you. I thought you were staying with your folks all weekend."

"That was the plan, but then I realized it was a bad plan. Felt like I should probably be here with you. Talk about this weird thing that's been going on between us all week." When Sloan's mouth twisted up in the corner, he knew he hadn't imagined the shitty feeling that had been digging under his skin. There was tension between them. Sloan gently set down the flowers and her laptop, then she pulled her knees up to her chest.

"We just had our first thing, didn't we?" she said.

"Yeah, I think we did."

"Not a fight, but a thing."

"Yeah, it was a thing." Rafe reached over few inches and gave her leg a light squeeze over the covers. "Here's a different thing I'm working on."

"Tell me."

"Needing space and wanting to give space. When emotions are running high, no matter the cause."

"Oh, yeah. That is tough. I wanted to climb up your ass all week, but I didn't want to seem needy."

"Is ass climbing a sign of neediness?"

"Yeah," Sloan laughed. "It's the number one symptom."

"I'll keep an eye out for it. I think I'm starting to love you a little bit, Dr. Copeland," he said, finally feeling like he was telling the whole truth.

"I'm starting to love you a little bit too." Rafe leaned up and pressed his lips to hers in a lingering kiss. When he pulled back, that light had returned to her eyes. The light he'd seen the first time he'd made her laugh. He knew then that they could do this.

"I'm glad you came back," she said.

"I am too." Rafe kissed her again. "Do you want an extra set of hands at the birthday party tomorrow?"

"No, but I would like my boyfriend there with me."

"I think we can make that happen."

"So, are you gonna stay there on the floor or do you want to get in this bed and cuddle me good?"

Rafe stood, moving Sloan's computer and the flowers to the far nightstand. He stepped out of his jeans and climbed between the sheets with her. They hadn't had the conversation about new sleeping arrangements yet, but for now Rafe knew he was exactly where he wanted to be.

Epilogue

Three years later…

Sloan was gonna come. Again.

When Monica had said she and Joe wanted to take Addison and Avery for the weekend, Sloan completely rearranged her mental plan for the weekend. Priority number one, leave the seminar on heart disease, break the sound barrier getting home and snuggle her sweet baby boy. Rowan was almost four months old, but that didn't stop Sloan from wanting to spend every minute getting high off that soft, new baby smell.

Priority number two, get her man between those sheets.

The last three years had gone by in a beautiful blur, especially after Drew realized his outburst had been caught on tape. The phone calls stopped and he finally agreed to Sloan's new custody terms. Addison and Avery would only see him if they wanted to. For a few months, they were completely on board with never seeing Drew again. Between them, they decided their grandmother Susan was more than welcome to come to L.A. and visit whenever she liked, but checking in with Drew via FaceTime once a month was all the contact they wanted with their father. That suited Sloan just fine.

With Drew mostly out of her hair, she finally felt like she could focus on her relationship with Rafe without worrying about Drew trying to ruin things. Without his intrusions, things between them moved pretty fast. It was a little awkward at first, explaining to people the particulars of their relationship, but after two weeks, the girls sorted out the dilemma for them. Rafe was their mom's boyfriend. The nanny bit was just a formality. Six months later, Rafe quit. The next morning, he proposed. Everything about it was perfect, including Addison and Avery's reaction to finding out that Rafe was finally going to be their dad. Their stay-at-home dad.

And not that he needed to, but Sloan appreciated that Rafe talked to her whole family about his intentions. Told them how much he cared for her and her girls, and how ready he was to move on with their life together. Sloan couldn't have been happier with the way her parents and her siblings welcomed him into their family. Rafe and her dad got along great. They texted each other all the time and she'd have to hand over the phone at least once a week so they could talk about sports and her dad's sudden interest in Harleys.

She was just as happy with how Hope and Gracie were over the moon to call her their sister-in-law and how quickly Monica and Joe snapped into ideal grandparent mode. Joe and her dad had also become fast friends. It was kinda cute. More than anything though, Sloan loved to see just how happy Addison and Avery were. She finally felt like she'd assembled the right kind of village for them. New family, more friends. Everything felt right.

Monica had a full weekend at Disneyland planned for the girls and while Sloan would be eager to see them come Sunday night, for now, she enjoying her quiet house. Well, quiet beyond the sounds of pure pleasure that she couldn't hold back.

"Babe," she moaned, driving her head back into the pillow. Her eyes squeezed shut when she felt his lips travel up the column of her neck, his cock pumping in and out of her. They had all weekend and she'd meant for them to take it slow, but one brush of her hand against his denim-covered cock had flipped his switched. She was still half dressed when he pushed inside her wet, aching pussy. He'd been eager to get her alone too. They'd take it slow the next round.

"Come," he groaned in her ear.

"Oh, babe. Please." Her hands trailed over his back, careful not to touch his most recent piece, three stars low on his left shoulder—one for Addison, one for Avery and one for baby Rowan. He'd add to it if and when they decided to add to their family.

Rafe's hand traveled down her thigh and hitched her knee up to her shoulder. That was all it took, the perfect angle for his perfect cock to stroke her in just the right way. Sloan came apart, her own desperate whimpers the only sound that she could hear. Rafe started moving faster, pumping into her throbbing pussy harder and harder, driving her body up the bed until she had to reach up and stop her head from hitting the headboard.

More tremors rolled through her. The intense pleasure started to subside. She wanted more. Sloan's hand went to the back of Rafe's neck and she pulled him down, sealing her lips to his as she started to ride him harder from underneath. He broke from their kiss, pressing his forehead to hers.

"Fuck, baby." She felt it then, his cock kicking and twitching insider her, filling her up with his cum. Another orgasm rolled through her.

He moved off of her and collapsed in the sheets. Sloan's eyes slowly opened when his hand slid over the map of stretch marks on her stomach. She rolled into him, pressing rough kisses to his shoulder.

"We're gonna fuck around and have another baby," he groaned.

"Oh, and I'm sure you'll hate that." Rafe wanted to act like he didn't text literally everyone they knew *I HAVE A SON* minutes after Rowan was cleaned and given the skin-to-skin contact that Sloan had insisted upon. Rafe doted on Addison and Avery, but the man was a pure fool over his baby boy.

He lifted his head and shot Sloan a weak attempt at a disgusted look. "Dr. Copeland, I can't help it if fatherhood looks good on me."

Sloan laughed, then made a fart noise with her tongue. "Right. Can I tell you what I'm thinking right now?"

"You don't know what you would do without my supreme lovemaking skills?"

"No, you ass. Though the dick is quality and I do appreciate it."

Rafe leaned up and gave her a quick kiss on the lips. "Thanks, baby."

"I wish we had a mini fridge up here so I could go ham on that leftover mac and cheese without getting out of bed."

Before Rafe could weigh in on light appliances in the bedroom, a cry came over the baby monitor. Sloan grabbed the tablet off her nightstand and sure enough, Rowan was fussing in his crib. There was a split second where she thought he would settle down on his own, but he was just getting started. He cranked out a louder, more pitiful cry.

"Fuck yeah. My buddy's up." Rafe hopped off the bed and pulled on his boxers.

"Change him or bring him to me. I don't want no fuckery in this dancery," Sloan teased.

"Ohhh," Rafe winced as he backed out of the room. "Sorry. He slept through a whole Brownie meeting like a champ yesterday. I told him he could stay up tonight and watch the game."

Sloan rolled her eyes and then edged off the bed as her husband walked down the hall toward the nursery. She stepped into the bathroom to bring herself all the way back down to Earth after three mind-blowing orgasms. She used the restroom and cleaned up, then changed into her pajamas just as Rafe came strolling into their bedroom, Rowan in his arms.

"Blew out that diaper, but I think we're good now." Sloan met them in the middle of the room and took Rowan from Rafe.

"Oh hello, my baby. Hello," she cooed, before she looked back up at Rafe. "Babe."

"Babe."

"Seventy-five cents if you'll run downstairs and get me that mac and cheese. And one of those key lime bars." Damn, her man could cook.

"I'll settle for twenty-five cents and that thing you do with your thumb," he countered.

"Oooooh, deal."

"Hot or cold?"

"Hmmm hot. Thank you."

"You got it."

After Rafe disappeared down the hall, she sat on the bed with Rowan, rocking him back to sleep. She picked up her phone and checked her texts. Xeni's aunt had recently passed away. Xeni just wanted to grieve, but speculation on the contents of her aunt's will had her family at each other's throats again.

She'd flown to upstate New York to scatter her aunt's ashes by her favorite creek and to figure out what to do with her three thousand square foot Colonial. She'd been quiet in their group chat, but she'd been keeping Sloan updated in their own text chain. She'd been quiet most of the day, though. Sloan clicked on the "3" near Xeni's name.

She almost fainted. She had to read the texts several times, but they still didn't make sense and Sloan had no freaking clue how to respond. She lay Rowan down in the cradle of her crossed legs and looked even harder at the screen, like the words would magically rearrange themselves.

Rafe came strolling back into the room. "I think I'm ready for a dog," he announced. In the back of her mind, Sloan could picture Rafe walking around the neighborhood, wearing Rowan in his chest carrier, the two of them being tugged down the street by some big, dopey mutt on a leash. She'd focus on how cute that vision was when she got to the bottom of her current mystery.

Rafe set down her food, then stroked her shoulder. "Hey, what's up?"

"Um, Xeni just texted me."

"How's she holding up? Is she still cleaning out her aunt's place?"

"I—I think so. I—she got married today."

"What? To who?!"

"Some Scottish guy named Mason."

Acknolwedgements

I must thank the following people in exact this order:

My parents
Holley Trent
My editor, T
Dr. Plantilla
Janet Eckford
My nieces and nephews
That girl I babysat one time in high school. I literally don't remember your name, but in my mind it's Addison. You were a really cool 5 year old.
All my writerly friends and the gals at The Ripped Bodice, for their on-going support.
Serena Williams

Author's Note

Let's talk about Loose Ends. What is this Loose Ends madness you're talking about, lady?!?! you might say.

Well I'll tell you, lovely reader. Over the years I've introduced a few supporting characters who deserve their very own happily ever after. While reading Rafe and Sloan's love story you might have seen Meegan pop up. She's in SATED, HAVEN and WRAPPED. Meegan deserves her own true love. As does Mason, Silas's Scottish cousin from SANCTUARY.

And speaking of cousins, I think it would be great to finally catch up with Meegan's cousin, Duke Stone and his on and off again lady love, Daniella from the SO SWEET trilogy. It'll take some time, but one by one, I will bring all these love birds together with the endings they need.

Up next is Mason and Sloan's all-star bestie, Xeni. Get ready. It's gonna be loads of fun!

xoxo Rebekah

About The Author

Rebekah Weatherspoon is freaking exhausted.

Come on by and get to know more about Rebekah on her Facebook, Twitter, or Tumblr. You can find more stories by Rebekah at rebekahweatherspoon.com

Twitter: @rdotspoon

Instagram.com/rebekahweatherspoon

www.rebekahweatherspoon.com
author@rebekahweatherspoon.com

9 781724 106506